"You think I'm a wolf?" he drawled lazily. "Of the big bad variety?"

"Aren't you?" she prevaricated.

"Not these days." Something flashed in the golden eyes and was gone. "Although I won't say I'd be able to resist doing this occasionally."

His lips had taken hers before she could do anything about it. It was a confident kiss, firm and sexy, his mouth exploring hers with an expertise that was far from chaste. He broke the kiss before she regained enough control to finish it.

"You prove you're not a wolf by kissing me?" she asked, proud of the slightly amused note she managed to inject into her tone, hiding her trembling hands in her lap.

"Absolutely. A wolf wouldn't have stopped at a kiss...."

HELEN BROOKS was born and educated in Northampton, England. She met her husband at the age of sixteen and thirty-five years later the magic is still there. They have three lovely children and four beautiful grandchildren.

Helen began writing in 1990 as she approached that milestone of a birthday—forty! She realized that her two teenage ambitions (writing a novel and learning to drive) had been lost amid babies and family life, so she set about resurrecting them. Her first novel was accepted after one rewrite, and she passed her driving test (the former was a joy and the latter an unmitigated nightmare).

Helen is a committed Christian and fervent animal lover. She finds time is always at a premium, but somehow fits in walks in the countryside with her husband and their Irish terrier, meals out followed by the cinema or theater, reading, swimming and visiting with friends. She also enjoys sitting in her wonderfully therapeutic, rambling old garden in the sun with a glass of red wine (under the guise of resting while thinking, of course!).

Since becoming a full-time writer Helen has found her occupation to be one of pure joy. She loves exploring what makes people tick and finds the old adage "truth is stranger than fiction" to be absolutely true. She would love to hear from any readers, care of Harlequin Presents.

SNOWBOUND SEDUCTION
HELEN BROOKS

~ Christmas Surrender ~

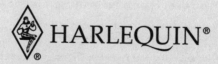

HARLEQUIN®

TORONTO • NEW YORK • LONDON
AMSTERDAM • PARIS • SYDNEY • HAMBURG
STOCKHOLM • ATHENS • TOKYO • MILAN • MADRID
PRAGUE • WARSAW • BUDAPEST • AUCKLAND

Recycling programs
for this product may
not exist in your area.

ISBN-13: 978-0-373-52794-6

SNOWBOUND SEDUCTION

First North American Publication 2010.

SNOWBOUND SEDUCTION

CHAPTER ONE

SURELY the run-up to Christmas wasn't meant to be like this? Driving rain, a bitter wind and everyone looking as though they could do murder. Children all over the world were opening the first little window of their Advent calendars today; there should be excitement and anticipation and a warm snuggly feeling for them at least, even if snow wasn't provided.

Rachel Ellington looked after the grim-faced mother with two screaming toddlers and a baby in a pushchair who had just elbowed her out of the way with such force it had hurt. And the harassed mother wasn't the only one with a face like thunder. The pavement was full of sullen schoolchildren with huge bags and even huger attitude; power-dressed commuters of both sexes hunched against the spray from passing traffic as they used their umbrellas like weapons; and a group of students jostling each other in a manner that suggested a fight might break out as they waited in a bus queue that stretched for ever.

Rachel glanced in the shop window she was passing and an enormous Father Christmas with a sack of gaily wrapped presents and a somewhat hideous grin stared back at her. It had been there since October, along with the fairy-lights and tinsel and Christmas tree.

Of course, that was half the trouble. The TV advertisements and shops and all levels of commerce began to whip up seasonal jollity so far in advance that by the beginning of December it was all used up. She grimaced as she realized she sounded just like her mother. But it was *true*, she thought, trying to ignore the drips of freezing water trickling down her neck. She'd forgotten her umbrella this morning—again.

She wouldn't go as far as her mother, who advocated a return to the days when the tree was dressed and decorations put up not an hour before Christmas Eve, and children should be presented with a stocking containing an orange, apple and nuts, along with a shiny coin and one present only, but there was something to be said for the old days when the latest 'must-have' toy costing an arm and a leg had been unheard of. And when a man saying 'I love you' meant more than just a nicety before getting you into bed.

She stood stock still as she realized what she'd just thought, causing major chaos for a moment as the people behind cannoned into her and each other.

Where had that little piece of cynicism sprung from? she asked herself as she apologised all round and started walking again. She was over Giles, she had been for months. And after the first caustic, devastating weeks in the summer when she had felt the whole world knew she'd been taken for a fool by the man she'd thought she'd be spending the rest of her life with, she'd become aware Giles had hurt her pride more than her heart. Which had caused her a few more sleepless nights. How could she imagine herself madly in love to the point of accepting his proposal of marriage one minute, and then be glad he was out of her life the next? It was positively scary when you thought about it.

Not that it had exactly been the next minute, she

qualified silently. She'd endured a few hellish weeks before that had come about, crying herself to sleep each night and losing nearly a stone in weight, which had given her a scrawny alleycat look. Already too thin by her own estimation it had been the spur she'd needed to start eating again, and she'd indulged in chocolate éclairs and other calorie-packed treats by the bucketful until her modest curves were back. Jennie and Susan, her flatmates, had been green with envy, which had been infinitely preferable to their pity of the preceding weeks.

As she turned off the main thoroughfare into the maze of side streets that eventually led to the tiny mews in Kensington where her flat was situated, a gust of wind and rain almost blew her off her feet. She normally enjoyed the brisk fifteen-minute walk home from the office but tonight was an ordeal. She should have travelled by tube but she had an aversion to the underground at the best of times, and a rainy December day with damp bodies steaming and lethal umbrellas by the hundreds definitely *wasn't* the best of times to journey in one of the packed rush-hour trains.

By the time she turned the key in the lock of the door of the downstairs flat she'd shared with her two best friends since the three of them had left university five years before, she was soaked to the skin. Her hair was plastered to her scalp, her mascara had run in rivulets down her cold cheeks and she was frozen to the marrow. She wanted nothing more than to lie in a scalding-hot bath for an hour with a glass of wine and a good book, and as she was always home long before Jennie and Susan, there was no reason she shouldn't.

She almost fell into the small square hall and stood for a moment with her eyes shut. Today had been a foul day altogether. After leaving university with a very acceptable 2.1 in business studies and marketing, she had obtained a post as assistant to the marketing manager of a fast-food chain. The pay was excellent and she knew her strengths were a keen awareness of client needs and a very good business sense, along with a natural flair for organising and planning. Unfortunately, on the latest project the sales team had failed to adequately follow up their part of the master plan, but due to a catalogue of half-truths and downright lies, it had been she who'd been left with egg on her face when the whole job had collapsed.

Rachel pulled off her sodden coat and kicked off her shoes, the memory of her manager Jeff's face when he'd taken her to task earlier that afternoon humiliatingly vivid. He'd been livid, having had a roasting from the managing director himself, and hadn't listened to a word she'd said in her defence.

She had entered the marketing world knowing promotion could be fast, but her chosen career was not for the faint-hearted: pressures were intense and security was mostly non-existent. She had been earmarked to take on Jeff's role when he transferred to the northern branch of the company early in the new year, but whether that would happen now was anyone's guess.

She frowned fiercely. All in all, she wouldn't be sad to see the back of this year and Christmas was going to be an endurance test. She had met Giles at a daytime Christmas party her firm had held for clients past and present the previous year, and they'd had their first date that same evening. This Christmas was going to give rise to some unwelcome memories.

'Hi, there.'

The deep male voice caused her to jump violently,

and as an involuntary gasp left her lips, she looked up to see a tall, dark stranger standing in the doorway of the sitting room. Her heart thumping so hard she put a hand to her chest to contain it, she bit out, 'Who on earth are you and what are you doing in my flat?' as her mind raced. What was within reach to defend herself with? Only her handbag, and much as she loved the sweet little red bow bag Jennie and Susan had bought her for her last birthday, it was hardly the stuff to strike terror into a burglar's heart.

There had been a spate of break-ins in the area over the last months and always when the householders were at work. Only last week one occupant of the mews had returned home to find her place being ransacked and the assailant had turned very nasty.

'Hey, it's OK.' The male voice was lazy. 'Don't panic.'

As he moved a pace or two towards her, Rachel felt in her bag for her perfume. 'This is a pepper spray and you come one step closer and you're getting it in the face,' she grated with more aggression than she was feeling. In truth she was scared to death. He was so big and broad. She hadn't turned the hall light on when she'd come in and he'd clearly just put a lamp on in the sitting room because the chink of light coming through the half-open door was so dim it merely shrouded him in shadow. Nevertheless, she could see she'd stand no chance.

'Let me give you a tip,' he said mildly. 'If you're going to use something like pepper spray, it's best not to give a warning. The element of surprise is crucial.'

He was now so close she could see his features and she received her second shock of the evening. As burglars went, this one was to die for. She already knew he was tall and dark, now add handsome multiplied by ten. Black hair, straight nose, firm sensual lips, and his eyes…She stared into the heavily lashed golden-brown gaze almost mesmerized. Pulling herself together, she said icily, 'Now, look here—'

'The name's Zac Lawson.' He said it as though it would clarify everything, and when she still continued to hold herself tense and at the ready, he added, 'Jennie's cousin? She called you and Susan earlier to explain.'

'Explain?' she echoed a little vacantly. The tawny eyes were compelling. *Too* compelling, a separate part of her mind stated ominously. Whoever he was, this man had more than his fair share of magnetism. Just like Giles. And like Giles, she had the feeling he'd use it to his advantage without any compunction whatsoever. Not reassuring in the circumstances.

'Have you checked your mobile recently?' he said patiently.

A little too patiently, Rachel thought critically. His voice carried more than a touch of long-suffering in its velvet depths. And, of course, today *would* be the day she'd turned her mobile off when she'd been called in to Jeff's office for her dressing-down and forgotten to turn it on again.

Stiffly, she said, 'I've been extremely busy.'

He nodded. A fairly benign action and his face was quite impassive, so why she should find the movement so offensive Rachel wasn't quite sure. Perhaps it was his resigned air?

'I'm Jennie's cousin,' he said again in the same patient tone. 'Our families lived in the same street while we were growing up so we saw a lot of each other before my parents moved to Canada when I was sixteen and Jennie was eleven. I'm over here on business for three weeks, and when I rang Jennie to say hi she insisted I have dinner with you all tonight.'

That explained the smoky, sexy burr to his voice. She hadn't been able to place the accent, it was so slight, but it added to his overall attraction a hundredfold. Not that she was attracted to him, she added hastily. She'd had her fill of arrogant, handsome charmers and Jennie's cousin seemed full of himself.

'I called in at Jennie's office and picked up her key earlier—she insisted the flat was a better place to chill out after the flight than a hotel room,' he continued lazily. 'I'm afraid I've been dead to the world on the sofa.'

Rachel forced a stiff smile. 'That's fine.' Remembering her manners, she added, 'Can I get you a drink?' as she reached out and switched on the light.

She became conscious of several things at the same time. Jennie's cousin was even more devastatingly gorgeous now she could see him properly. There was a touch of grey in the black hair above his ears but it only increased the male magnetism, and the golden gaze was truly spellbinding in the bright light. She had never seen another person with eyes like his. Secondly, those same eyes were surveying her with definite amusement. Thirdly, his clothes—not to mention the gold Rolex on one tanned wrist—screamed wealth and taste, and lastly—but most importantly—she looked like something the cat wouldn't deign to drag in.

Ignoring the puddle of water that had formed at her feet, she kept the smile on her face through sheer willpower. 'A glass of wine?' she persevered. 'Or I think we have a bottle of brandy somewhere. Or perhaps you'd prefer coffee or tea?' she added graciously, the effect being somewhat spoilt when she shivered convulsively and then sneezed three times.

His voice had gentled to the tone one would use with a very young child. 'Why don't you go and change out of those wet clothes while I fix us *both* some coffee? I think of the two of us you're in need more than me right at this moment.'

She couldn't deny it, with her teeth chattering loud enough to wake the dead. Besides which, she wanted nothing more than to escape those lethal eyes and make herself presentable. She had never fooled herself she could compete with Jennie's dark-eyed voluptuous beauty or Susan's delicate blonde appeal. Her own brown hair and blue eyes were fairly nondescript in her opinion, but looking like a drowned rat was something else.

Clinging onto the shreds of her dignity, Rachel nodded brightly. He had said and done nothing wrong, not really, and she didn't know why she had taken such an instant dislike to Jennie's cousin, but she had. Nevertheless, he was a guest and she knew her manners. 'Thank you. The coffee and sugar pots are on the breakfast bar and there's a fruit cake in the cake tin in the cupboard. Side plates and mugs are—'

'I'll find everything. Why don't you have a hot bath?'

Now his voice was distinctly soothing as he interrupted her and it made her want to kick him. Feeling more than a little unnerved by the strength of her own feelings and completely out of her depth, she decided retreat was the only option. 'I won't be long,' she managed as she left for the bathroom. 'Please make yourself at home.' As if he hadn't already.

Rachel forwent the hot bath for a warm shower,

stuffing her wet clothes in the laundry basket before pulling on the towelling robe she kept on a peg behind the bathroom door and padding through to the bedroom she shared with Jennie to dry her hair. When the three of them had moved into the flat it had been agreed Susan would occupy the tiny second bedroom owing to the fact she snored—loudly.

The ravages of her make-up having been removed in the bathroom, she applied fresh eye shadow and mascara before drying her hair whilst sitting at the small dressing table. She left her thick shoulder-length hair loose, she hadn't got time to fiddle with it, and quickly pulled on a pair of jeans and a warm sweater, surveying herself in the full-length mirror on the wall before she left the room.

Better, but then, anything would be better than the sight she had presented in the hall. What must he have thought? And then she answered herself sharply. It didn't matter what Zac Lawson thought. Not one little bit. And as soon as she possibly could after dinner, she was claiming a headache and leaving the rest of them to it. Polite conversation she could do without.

She could smell coffee when she exited the bedroom and as though he had some sort of X-ray vision that could see through brick walls, Zac appeared in the doorway to the sitting room. 'Just in time,' he said, as though she were the guest and he was the householder. 'Come and have some coffee and cake.'

Rachel found she was gritting her teeth as she followed him into the room, and then tried to compose her features into a more acceptable expression as he turned and indicated the tray on the coffee table. 'There was milk and cream in the fridge so I brought both, along with a tin of coffee whitener I found.'

How thorough. Knowing she was being uncharacter-istically bitchy, Rachel cleared her throat. 'I take mine black.'

'Really?' He stared at her as he passed her a mug.

She'd surprised him. Good. She had the feeling women didn't surprise Zac Lawson too often. He had the confident aura of a man who had the world in general pretty much taped.

When she cut them both a piece of cake and her slice was as large as his, she knew she'd surprised him for the second time in as many minutes. She answered the raised eyebrow with a shrug. 'Fast metabolism.'

One corner of his slightly stern and very sexy mouth twisted. 'I bet the other girls love you when they're chomping on lettuce and you're tucking into the full McCoy and still looking like a model, fast metabolism or not.'

Looking like a model? Was he being sarcastic? She stared at him. He had the sort of face it was impossible to read. Coolly, she said, 'Hardly.'

'They don't mind?'

He was definitely being deliberately obtuse. 'I meant I hardly look like a model,' she said even more coolly, taking a bite of cake and hoping he'd take the hint and leave well alone.

He settled back in the comfy armchair that faced the sofa where she sat, arms stretched out along the back of the seat and one leg crossed over the other knee. It was a very masculine pose. He was a very masculine man. The tawny eyes moved over her face. She could feel them even though she was concentrating on the plate on her lap.

'You look perfect model material to me,' he said mildly.

Was he teasing her or flirting or what? Whatever, she so wasn't doing this. Regretting that she'd let him see he'd got to her and wishing she'd just let it go in the first place, Rachel forced a smile. 'Well, I haven't been spotted by a talent scout to date and I'm perfectly happy with the day job.' Even to herself she sounded overly facetious. A little desperately now, she added, 'What is it you do, by the way?'

He didn't comment on the clumsy change of conversation. Demolishing half his slice of cake with one bite, he chewed and swallowed at leisure before he said, 'I work in the family glass-making business back home in Canada. Have done since uni.'

Unexpected. In spite of herself, Rachel was intrigued. 'Really? That's a very old industry, isn't it?' She'd had him down as a modern whizz-kid, all bells and whistles and something mega in the city.

'It goes back some,' he agreed lazily, finishing his cake before he continued, 'The Canadian side of the family have had their own business for over a century and it's been handed down through the generations. Most glass-making firms, like other old industries, have been taken over by large manufacturing groups. We're one of the few family businesses still going, which is the main reason my father moved us to Canada when I was a youth. He'd had a falling out with his father—my grandfather—when he was a young man and left Canada for England. My grandfather had his first heart attack when I was sixteen and my grandmother begged my father to return. There was a kind of a reconciliation and, as my father was their only child, he agreed to return permanently and take over.'

Intrigued, she said, 'What was the falling out about?' before blushing violently as she realised how nosy that sounded. 'I'm sorry,' she added hastily before he could speak. 'It's none of my business. You really don't have to answer that.'

'No problem. My father met my mother when she was holidaying in Canada and it was one of those rare instant for-ever things. My grandfather thought my father ought to marry the daughter of some friends of theirs, apparently the two sets of parents had planned it for years. The girl was willing, my father wasn't. He'd already made his feelings plain before he met my mother, but my grandfather wasn't used to being thwarted. He's an irascible old man when he gets the bit between the teeth, as he often does.'

'He's still alive?'

'Very much so. Three heart attacks to date, mainly, so my grandmother insists, because of his temper. Anyway, there were harsh words on both sides and my father followed my mother to England and married her. It was twenty-five years before my grandfather and father spoke again. The Lawson males are a stubborn lot, it's in the genes.' He smiled.

She didn't doubt it. There was something in the square jaw that told her Zac was no different from the rest of them.

It was cosy in the small sitting room, which was still dimly lit. Rain was lashing at the window and the flickering flames from the gas fire cast the hard male face into moving planes and angles. Rachel shivered, though not from cold. There was something infinitely... unsettling about Jennie's Canadian cousin. Undoubtedly he was very sure of himself, he exuded an arrogance that set her teeth on edge, but it was more than that—quite what, she didn't know.

'So you're over here on business for a while?' she said

when the silence became uncomfortable. On her part at least. Zac appeared perfectly relaxed as he finished his coffee.

'Uh-huh.' He smiled, the tawny eyes glittering in the dim light. 'That cake's pretty good.'

She took the broad hint and cut him another hefty slice. As she did so his mobile phone rang and he glanced at it before saying, 'Do you mind if I answer this?'

'Of course not.' At least it would delay having to make conversation for a while. As she rose to give him some privacy, he said quickly, 'No, please stay,' before speaking into the phone, 'Hi, Sarah. How are things going there?'

The girlfriend? She muttered something about things to see to in the kitchen and made her escape. Of course, he could be married. He wasn't wearing a ring but lots of men didn't.

They were having shepherd's pie for dinner, which Jennie had prepared the night before, it being her turn on kitchen duty that week, and there was ample for four. Glancing at the clock, Rachel put the pie in the oven and sliced some fresh carrots and broccoli, trying not to strain her ears to catch what was being said in the sitting room. She heard him laugh, a warm, rich sound, and paused for a moment before reaching for the pot of double cream in the fridge and tipping it into a bowl. Once the electric mixer was going, it drowned out any sound from the sitting room, and when the cream peaked she put the finishing touches to the raspberry trifle Jennie had designated for dessert. As she did so, Zac appeared in the doorway.

'You needn't have left,' he said quietly. 'It was only my secretary reporting on things at the office.'

His secretary? Things had sounded mighty cosy; perhaps he mixed business and pleasure? 'I needed to see to the dinner,' she said as she gave herself a mental slap. What business was it of hers if Zac was sleeping with his secretary? Giles had been sleeping with his too but the irony there was that she was his wife—a little fact he'd omitted to mention when he'd met her. And when he'd proposed. She'd only found out he was married when his wife had turned up on her doorstep one evening, having learnt of their relationship through a friend of a friend of a friend.

She didn't know if it made it better or worse that she wasn't the only woman he'd fooled about with since his marriage eight years before, but she had believed his wife absolutely when she'd told her the cold facts. She was just amazed Melanie had stuck with him so long. Giles's wife had been *nice*, the sort of woman she could have been friends with in different circumstances. Much too nice for a rat like Giles.

'You OK?' Zac shifted in the doorway.

Too late she realised her always too-expressive face had given her away. 'Fine,' she said with a careless shrug, hoping he'd take himself back to the sitting room. 'I'll come and join you in a minute,' she added pointedly, turning to the dirty breakfast dishes in the sink and filling the washing-up bowl with hot, soapy water. 'The others should be back soon.'

To her horror he had joined her in the next moment, tea towel in hand. The kitchen wasn't large as it was, but with his height and breadth dwarfing her it had suddenly got a whole lot smaller. 'No.' It came out too sharply, and she modified her tone when she said, 'You're a guest. I wouldn't dream of letting you dry up,' hoping she didn't sound as flustered as she felt, although she knew it was a vain hope.

Looking relaxed and slightly amused, he murmured, 'I've no problem with working for my supper.'

'No, really, I mean it.' She stood guard over the dishes.

'So do I.' He smiled easily but his tone was cooler.

Rachel jutted out her chin like a teenager. This was ridiculous. It was *her* kitchen. 'This is too small a room, only one person at a time works in here. We've got a rota...' That sounded silly. 'And,' she said truculently, 'I've got my own way of doing things.'

'How difficult is it to get it wrong when you dry dishes?'

'I'll bring you a glass of wine through in a minute,' she said, purposely not answering him, 'and Jennie will be home any moment. She'll expect you to be sitting watching TV.'

'I think she'd survive the shock nonetheless.'

It was useless arguing with him but neither was she going to give in. She was blowed if she was going to let another Giles tell her what to do. She stood, straight and stiff and without glancing at him until she heard him leave the kitchen. Then she let her body sag. Damn, damn, damn. Now she felt awful. She was never intentionally rude and he was Jennie's cousin after all, but why couldn't he take a hint? Irritating, awkward man.

Without considering what she was going to say, she marched through to the sitting room. He was standing with his back to the room looking out of the window into the dark, stormy night.

'I'm sorry,' she said without any preamble. 'I sounded rude and I didn't mean to be. It's just that—'

'You don't like me for some reason,' he finished for

her, turning round and pinning her with the golden gaze. 'Right?'

Lost for words, Rachel shook her head helplessly. 'I don't know you,' she prevaricated at last.

'No, you're right, you don't,' he said softly, but with an iron edge to his voice that hadn't been there before. 'If you *did* know me and you'd still come to that conclusion, it wouldn't matter.' He smiled, but it didn't reach his eyes. 'As it is, I guess it still doesn't matter, but I'd appreciate you trying to be civil this evening for Jennie's sake, if nothing else.'

Her temper rising, she stared at him. 'Of course I'll be civil. I told you, I didn't mean to be rude.' Her words were clipped, frosty. How dared he tell her what to do in her own home?

She thought she saw the hard mouth twitch for a moment. 'That's very reassuring.'

He was laughing at her again. How dared he? But the hot words quivering on her tongue fortunately never got said. Jennie chose that moment to open the front door of the flat, calling out, 'Zac? Are you here?' as she entered the hall.

Rachel saw her friend's eyes widen when they took in the tall handsome man her cousin had become, and then, in true Jennie style, she'd flung herself into Zac's arms and planted a smacking kiss on his mouth before he had a chance to object.

Not that he would have objected, Rachel told herself as she left them to it, murmuring something about opening a bottle of wine. Jennie was gorgeous with her black hair and dark brown eyes and the sort of Marilyn Monroe figure that turned men on from schoolboys to geriatrics. And she was between men at the moment, having just dumped her latest boyfriend. They never lasted long with Jennie, she bored easily.

When she re-entered the sitting room Jennie had drawn Zac down beside her on the sofa and was asking about the family, one hand resting on his arm as she gazed up into his face. Rachel knew that look. And when Jennie set her sights on a man they didn't stand a chance. It normally amused her when Jennie went into her femme fatale role. Tonight, though, she felt rattled and disturbed. She was careful to give no sign of her feelings when she poured the wine, filling the fourth glass on the tray when Susan's key sounded in the lock.

Susan joined them, slender, beautiful Susan with her white blonde hair and the face of an angel, smiling charmingly and saying all the right things as Jennie introduced her to Zac. And Zac was as charming back. He'd stood up when Susan had entered the room and now displayed the most perfect manners, his conversation witty and amusing as they sipped at their wine.

Rachel sat watching the other three and said little, she didn't need to. Jennie and Susan and Zac were getting on like a house on fire. She felt a growing sense of *déjà vu* but she didn't have to search her mind long for the cause. How often in the past, before she'd escaped the family home for university, had she sat and watched her two older sisters be the life and soul of the proceedings while she'd sat dumbly by? Dozens of times. Hundreds probably. And yet every time had hurt just as much.

After two sweet, girly, blonde little girls, her mother had decided her third child would be a boy to complete their perfect family, and her mother always got what she wanted. Except she'd had another girl. And this girl had been long and skinny with straight brown hair when she'd finally grown hair at the embarrassingly late age of eighteen months. Embarrassing for her mother, that was, Rachel thought grimly. She had been brought up on stories of how mortified her mother had been in producing such an ugly duckling. Or perhaps cuckoo in the nest was a better description. Lisa and Claire, her sisters, with only fifteen months between them, had always been inseparable, and she'd grown up feeling the odd one out in more ways than one. It wasn't until she'd met Jennie and Susan in the first week of university that she'd come to understand the meaning of true friendship and support from members of her own sex. The three of them had gelled instantly; it was her misfortune the other two were quite stunning.

Her forehead creased as she sipped at her wine, her gaze now inward looking. What would Freud say about her choice of friends? That she was unconsciously trying to right the wrongs of her childhood or that she'd been programmed to purposely seek out friends who would overshadow her? She mentally shook her head at the path her thoughts had taken, suddenly annoyed with herself and the self-psychoanalysis.

She and Jennie and Susan were genuine, rock-solid friends and had been from the first—it was as simple as that.

'I'd better see to the dinner.' Jennie jumped up in the next moment, flashing Rachel a smile as she added, 'Thanks for putting it on, Cinders.'

'Cinders?' Zac's eyes shot to Rachel's face. 'Why Cinders?'

As Zac immediately homed in on the nickname, Rachel could have kicked Jennie, who'd already sailed out of the room. It was Susan who said, a little uncomfortably, having seen Rachel's glare, 'It's just a pet name, that's all.'

'But *Cinders*?' There was a note in his voice that told Rachel he wasn't going to let this drop.

Silently calling Jennie every name under the sun, Rachel sighed before saying resignedly, 'I've two older sisters, that's all.'

'And you don't get on with them? Or are they ugly?'

Rachel stared hard at Zac and he stared back. She could tell he was trying to keep a straight face in view of her antagonism. 'I get on with them just fine and they are far from ugly.' The understatement of the year, she thought wryly. She had been foolish enough to follow her sisters to the same university and within days some wit had dubbed her Cinders, a tongue-in-cheek play on the fairy-tale. Somehow the nickname had stuck and within a couple of weeks everyone had forgotten her real name. Even Jennie and Susan had adopted it, but she knew with them it was said with warm affection. And she didn't mind. Normally.

The handsome brow wrinkled. 'Then why—?'

She shrugged as she rose to her feet. 'Lisa and Claire are outstandingly beautiful; I suppose someone thought it was clever. I'll just give Jennie a hand with the dinner.'

She left before he could make a comment.

CHAPTER TWO

RACHEL found dinner a trying affair. But not Jennie and Susan. They positively sparkled. In fact, Susan seemed to have completely forgotten she was on the verge of becoming engaged to her long-standing—and extremely patient—boyfriend, Henry. Rachel liked Henry and she didn't think he'd appreciate Susan's fluttering eyelashes as she gazed at Zac.

Still, it was none of her business.

She told herself this during Jennie's delicious shepherd's pie—that was another thing about Jennie, she was a fabulous cook—and also during dessert, which was equally fabulous. By the coffee and mints stage of the meal, her eyes felt gritty and her head ached. She had never felt so tense in the whole of her life. The trouble was, she was aware of Zac Lawson in a way she hadn't experienced before. Even when her eyes weren't directly on him—and she'd taken care that was the case for most of the time—she found herself registering every slight movement, every turn of his head or quirk of his lips. It was annoying and irritating but her nerves seemed sensitised to a humiliating degree in his presence. And for the life of her she didn't know why.

She had said very little throughout the meal but the other three had more than made up for her lack of conversation. She didn't think anyone had noticed her quietness, so it came as a shock when Zac turned to her, coffee cup in hand, and said softly, 'So, Rachel, I know Jennie's a fashion buyer and Susan works in a lab—what do you do?'

She tried to get beyond the fact that she felt the golden gaze was drawing her in and answer coherently. 'I'm in marketing.'

He nodded. 'Enjoy it?'

'Very much.' Her voice emerged in a husky croak and she quickly cleared her throat. 'I wouldn't want to do anything else.' Of course, she might have to if Jeff sacked her and wouldn't give her a reference after today's fiasco.

'What sort of thing are you involved in?' he asked, as though he really wanted to know and wasn't just being polite. Then again, he'd been equally interested in Jennie and Susan. He was clearly a man who could make the woman he was with—or in this case talking to—feel she was the only one who mattered. Giles had been the same. That type mostly were, she supposed.

She gave a brief—very brief—outline of her job and then rose to her feet before he could pursue the conversation. 'I hope you don't mind but I've got a headache,' she said, her gaze sweeping the three of them, 'and I think I'll turn in. It was nice meeting you, Zac.' She allowed her eyes to rest on him for the merest moment but it was enough to cause a quiver inside as the handsome face surveyed her. 'I hope your business here goes well and the trip is successful,' she added politely.

'Thank you, Rachel.' His voice was velvet smooth, but his eyes declared he was fully aware of the real reason she was retiring to her room and found it faintly amusing.

Well, he could laugh at her all he wanted but she *did* have a headache and she was blowed if she was going to sit there and endure another minute of his company. Her back stiff, hackles rising, she gave him an arctic smile and left the room as Jennie leaned forward and lightly touched his arm, bringing his attention back to her. 'You must come to dinner again tomorrow if you're free, Zac. You could come every night while you're here, as far as we're concerned. Isn't that right, Susan?'

She didn't wait to hear his reply, shutting the door on their tiny dining room-cum-study and standing in the hall for a moment as indignation swamped her. If that man was coming here every night, then she'd be eating out for the next three weeks. And this was *her* home as much as Jennie's—her friend should have consulted her before making such a sweeping statement.

Rachel was feeling ashamed of herself even before she reached the bedroom and her penance was to lie tossing and turning and straining her ears. She heard the others leave the dining room and go into the sitting room then some music filtered through, along with the low buzz of conversation and laughter. Giggly, we're-hanging-on-your-every-word laughter from Jennie and Susan, and a deep, rumbly male laugh now and again that made every nerve and sinew in her body stretch.

It was the longest two hours of her life before she heard the front door open and close, and then a few minutes later Jennie tiptoed into their room. A little while later, Jennie's steady regular breathing told Rachel her friend was fast asleep; likewise Susan, as the muted snores through the wall proclaimed. Not for the first time she wondered how someone as ethereal and beautifully delicate as Susan could produce such a sound.

She must have drifted off to sleep eventually because

she awoke at six o'clock, an hour before the alarm, after disturbing dreams she couldn't remember but which left her with an uneasy, unsettled feeling in the pit of her stomach. It was still dark when she made her way to the bathroom, deciding to have a long hot bath to soak away the stresses of the day before. She filled the tub and added plenty of her favourite bath oil. If ever there was a morning to pamper herself, this was it. She didn't know what she was going to face at work today, she told herself, and that was the reason—the only reason—for the butterflies in her stomach and the feeling that her world was out of kilter.

By seven o'clock she was dressed and made up and sitting at the table laid for three with a full coffee pot and a stacked plate of waffles, Jennie's favourite breakfast. Her atonement for the night before. Not that the others would have minded her leaving, they'd probably hardly noticed, the way they'd been focusing on Zac, but this made her feel better.

'Ooh, waffles, lovely.' Jennie padded into the dining room and plonked herself down at the table, reaching for the pot of honey and liberally dousing her first waffle. 'Why the treat? We normally only do this at weekends. Weekdays are toast and instant coffee. Not that I'm complaining, of course, far from it.'

'I couldn't sleep,' Rachel said airily, smiling at Susan who had just appeared and whose response to the waffles was a carbon copy of Jennie's. 'So I thought I'd spoil us all.'

Both her friends were in their pyjamas and still-tousled haired without a scrap of make-up, and both looked gorgeous. Rachel sighed unconsciously.

'What?' Susan glanced at her. 'What's the matter?'

She thought about prevaricating and then said honestly, 'I'd give my eye teeth to look like you two in the morning. Have either of you *ever* had blotchy morning skin or sticky-out hair or a spot that wasn't there the night before?'

'Loads of times.' Susan grinned at her and reached for a waffle. 'Sometimes I look like the wicked witch of the west.'

Liar, liar, pants on fire.

'Anyway, it was you Zac was asking about last night,' Susan continued casually, 'in spite of Jennie doing her best to persuade him they were kissing cousins.'

Rachel's heart stopped and then kick-started. She had to wait for a moment before she could control her voice enough to say, 'Asking what exactly?' in a faintly bored tone.

'The normal things. These waffles are gorgeous, by the way.'

The normal things? What on earth were the normal things? 'Like…?' Rachel prompted carefully.

'If there was a boyfriend around,' Jennie put in. 'Of course, he could just have been being friendly. We'd sort of filled him in about us.'

'Yes, I think it took Jennie all of a few seconds to make the point I was seeing Henry and she was fancy-free,' Susan said a touch acidly. 'Along with how she's just *dying* to see that new play at the Grecian theatre.'

Jennie grinned good-naturedly. 'A girl has to do what a girl has to do, and you must admit he's some sort of hunk. I don't remember him being so drop-dead gorgeous when we were children.'

'Probably because the last time you saw him you were a kid with pigtails and braces and more interested in horses than boys.' Susan was petrified of horses and had been frankly incredulous when Jennie had told them one day she had ridden all the time as a child and had had her own pony called Primrose.

'True.' Jennie started on her third waffle. 'But I'm very interested now and I haven't given up on Zac yet. I mean, as family it's my duty to show him around while he's here and look after him.' She tried an innocent smile that didn't fool anyone.

Susan spluttered half her waffle onto her plate. 'And we all know how you want to look after him,' she said lewdly, rolling her eyes. 'And cooking dinner for him is the tip of the iceberg.'

Jennie didn't deny it. 'I bet he's great in bed,' she said dreamily. 'Sexy, experienced but considerate, you know?'

Rachel found she couldn't sit and listen any longer. Abruptly, she said as she stood up, 'I had a disaster at work yesterday and I need to be in early. I'm not at all sure I'll still have a job soon, to be honest.'

'Oh, no.' Both girls were instantly all concern and comfort, and as she detailed what had happened they said the right things in the right places and were suitably scathing about the sales team. It helped how she was feeling. A bit.

As she left them, Rachel said offhandedly, 'Is Zac having dinner with us again tonight?' and hoped the jitters that had assailed her all morning since waking weren't evident in her voice.

'Nope, he's busy.' Jennie's voice brightened as she added, 'But I've got his number and I'll try later for tomorrow. I might suggest treating him to dinner at Alfredo's and then taking him to a nightspot. What do you think? Somewhere where the dance floor is small and cosy so we can get in the mood.'

'I take it you mean a nightspot followed by his hotel

room?' Susan winked at Rachel, who had paused in the doorway.

'Absolutely,' Jennie agreed cheerfully. 'Or just his hotel room.'

'Jennie, you're such an out-and-out tart.'

'I know. Tarts have all the fun.'

Rachel left the other two amiably chaffing each other but she wasn't smiling as she fetched her coat and handbag from her room. Jennie had never made any secret of the fact she slept with all her boyfriends and enjoyed sex, and although Susan was a little more choosy, she'd had a few partners too.

Here again she was the odd one out. She stared at her reflection in the long mirror on the bedroom wall. Jennie and Susan had thought it hilarious in their university days when she had said she was waiting for Mr Right before sleeping with a boy, but back then she had imagined he would come along before too long. And the truth of it was she had never met anyone who had made her pulse flutter and tempted her before Giles, so it hadn't been too difficult to hang onto the dream. She'd had lots of boyfriends before him and had enjoyed kissing and cuddling and a bit of petting, but whenever they'd pressed for more she had known she would regret it the next morning. It was just the way she was made. She'd long ago come to terms with the fact that she was an oddity in her group of friends.

Rachel frowned at the brown-haired girl in the mirror. She wanted it to be special with the man she fell in love with, a forever thing, something that meant more than words could explain, but after Giles she was wondering if love as she saw it even existed. And she didn't want to die an old maid.

What had kept her from sleeping with Giles? He'd

certainly pestered her enough in the last couple of months before he had proposed, and she had imagined herself in love with him, hadn't she? Her frown deepened. *Hadn't she?*

Yes, she had thought she loved him but something hadn't been quite…right. Even then some sixth sense must have been telling her he wasn't what he seemed, that he had been projecting an image he'd thought she'd wanted him to be.

She shut her eyes tightly, biting on her lip. Jennie was right and she was wrong. She should have slept with every Tom, Dick and Harry and had fun; sex was just a pleasant pastime between a man and a woman and didn't have to be an emotional forever thing. It didn't have to lead to marriage and babies.

Her eyes opened. But it would need to for her. She simply couldn't imagine opening her life and her body to a man and then cheerfully waving goodbye to him whenever the relationship ended. Jennie could. She couldn't. End of story. She didn't want to go through life alone but if she had to, she would. Loads of women concentrated on their career these days and chose autonomy and had rich and fulfilling lives. She just hadn't imagined that was the way her life would go when she had been younger.

She took a deep breath. She could hear Jennie singing a pop song in the bathroom and smiled wryly to herself. The world did indeed 'rain down men' on Jennie; no sooner had her friend disposed of one man than another took his place. She envied her. Oh, how she envied her. No heart-searching, no agonising, no emotional baggage. Jennie ate when she was hungry, drank when she was thirsty and slept with a man when she wanted sex. And

Jennie never felt that she was a failure and had missed the boat in a hundred and one ways.

At the end of the day Rachel still had a job, so she supposed she could count it a success. She'd gone for lunch with a group of girls from the office but although she had joined in the conversation and acted naturally, part of her—annoyingly—had kept repeating a post-mortem of the night before.

If she analysed it, she couldn't quite understand why Zac Lawson had got under her skin the way he had. It hadn't been so much what he'd said or done as the way he'd said and done it, she told herself. A certain inflexion, a tone of voice, a look, and perfectly mundane words could have a whole different meaning. Even simple words like 'Thank you' could change according to the way someone spoke or the expression on their face—it could be grateful or sarcastic or wry or a whole host of things. But however much she tried to wriggle out of it, she had to admit she'd been uncharacteristically belligerent from the second she'd set eyes on Jennie's cousin. And she didn't like herself for it.

She sighed as she pulled on her coat at the end of the day, after switching off her computer and tidying her desk. If she saw Zac again she'd be politely friendly, she determined, for Jennie's sake. She didn't like him—in fact, she'd never met a man she liked less—but that couldn't be helped and Jennie needn't know. And it wasn't as if he would be around for long anyway; she could force herself to be civil to the poor man for the short time he was in the country if their paths crossed.

It was raining again when she walked down the steps of the office building and her umbrella was safely propped up in the hallstand at the flat. In the couple of years since she'd bought it, she'd only used it a handful of times, she reflected ruefully.

She had reached the pavement before she saw him, leaning nonchalantly against the wall of the building next door.

'No umbrella again?' The velvet voice with its faintest of Canadian undertones mocked her wide-eyed surprise. As he reached her, he sheltered her under his own black monster of an umbrella. 'Do you actually *like* getting wet through?'

He'd slipped a casual arm round her waist as he'd drawn her out of the rain and she was aware of feeling very feminine against his broad-shouldered bulk. Then the dumbness brought about by shock faded and she found her voice. Carefully pulling back so there was a couple of inches between them, she said tightly, 'What are you doing here?'

'Isn't it obvious? Rescuing a damsel in distress.'

'I'm not in distress.'

'You would be if you walked home in this lot.'

The rain was coming down faster now, thudding on top of the umbrella in great icy drops that annoyingly backed up his statement. Rachel swallowed hard. He smelt divine. Whatever his aftershave was, it was worth every penny. 'How do you know where I work?'

Stupid question, she thought in the next millisecond.

His dry voice backed up the thought when he murmured, 'Jennie. I rang her and asked for the address and told her I wanted to take you out to dinner.'

'But—' She stopped abruptly, warning herself to be careful.

'What?' His eyes under their thick black lashes surveyed her.

'Jennie said you'd told her last night you were busy this evening.' And she could just imagine Jennie's reaction to the news when Zac had phoned. She stared into the strong face, her gaze taking in a slight cleft in his chin she hadn't noticed the evening before. She shivered. But not with cold.

He shrugged. 'My plans changed. It happens.'

'I—I can't have dinner with you.' Don't stutter and stammer, for goodness' sake, she told herself disgustedly.

'Why not?' His tone was more interested than offended.

He was nothing if not direct. But there was no way she was going to be intimidated. She indicated her briefcase. 'I have work to do tonight and it can't wait.'

'That's OK, you can do it later.' He smiled, a slow, curving smile that made her stomach roll over and took the arrogance out of his declaration. 'You would eat at some time tonight, why not with me? And you'll work better on a full stomach. I do.'

Hotly aware that several of her co-workers were giving them interested glances as they passed, she muttered, 'Jennie's free tonight, ask her. I know she'd love to go to dinner with you.'

'I don't want to have dinner with Jennie, Rachel. I want to have dinner with you,' he said softly. 'And don't look at me as though I'm the Marquis de Sade. I'm suggesting dinner, that's all, and I promise you'll be safely delivered home later.'

Her mouth fell open and then snapped shut. How dared he? She was so taken aback by his effrontery she didn't know what to say for a moment. Suggesting she was some nervous teenager scared at the thought of dinner with a man! 'If we are talking straight here, you know full well why I won't have dinner with you,' she said tartly. 'It must have been obvious Jennie likes you, surely? I wouldn't do anything to upset or offend her.'

'And I like Jennie. She's my cousin, there are childhood memories and all that sentimental stuff. But I have no wish to date her, Rachel, and I won't pretend otherwise. I made that clear to Jennie today and she was quite philosophical about it, I promise. Her heart remains intact.'

He was laughing at her again—she knew it even if the tawny eyes were serious. She wished she had the will to turn round and walk away without another word, to cut him dead, but curiously she couldn't do it. Somehow she managed to make her voice cool and polite as she said, 'Nevertheless, I don't think dinner is a good idea.'

Part of her was still numb with disbelief that he *wanted* to have dinner with her, especially when Jennie had made it clear how she felt. And then a thought occurred. Maybe that was exactly why he *had* asked her? If he didn't fancy Jennie then the best way to make it clear was to take another woman out.

'I think dinner's a wonderful idea,' he said smoothly, 'but let's discuss it in comfort, shall we?'

Before she knew where she was he had bundled her into the taxi that had been waiting at the kerb. She hadn't realised it was Zac's and as he slid in beside her she was tempted to exit the other side, but something in the hard male face told her he would simply haul her back in. She wouldn't put anything past him, she told herself bitterly before she said, 'I'd like to go to the flat, please.' She glared at him defiantly.

'And you shall. Later.'

Rachel hated the mocking lift to his voice. She listened as he gave the name of a famous restaurant a few blocks away to the driver. It cost an arm and a leg to eat there.

'This could be termed kidnapping, you know,' she said stiffly.

His irritating eyebrows—irritating because they had a way of arching up in a manner guaranteed to provoke— rose. 'Surely not,' he murmured lazily, turning to survey her with one arm along the back of the seat behind her head. He was wearing a heavy black overcoat, which intensified his dark maleness, and Rachel breathed out carefully. 'I'm a stranger to your city and I'm asking you to spend a couple of hours with me over dinner, that's all. A good meal, a nice wine and a little conversation.'

Now he was making her feel like a worm. Deliberately, no doubt.

'If I had asked Jennie, she would have assumed the evening would end in bed. It would have sent all the wrong signals and maybe caused a problem. I didn't want that. But I did want some company. Is that so terrible?'

She stared at him and his eyebrows did it again. Knowing she'd been beaten by an expert, she gave it one last try. 'And what about the problem my having dinner with you might cause between Jennie and myself?'

He smiled a little grimly. 'Jennie knows you don't like me very much. I doubt she'll lose any sleep tonight.'

She could feel the colour flooding her cheeks but couldn't do anything about it. She wasn't going to deny it, though. After a moment, she said carefully, 'If you think that's how I feel, why would you want to spend some time with me?'

He tilted his head back and fixed her with the disturbingly beautiful eyes. Now he was so close she could see the golden brown had deep tawny flecks in it, like one of the big cats you saw on wildlife programmes. Combined with the thick black lashes, it made his eyes mesmerising.

'I like a challenge,' he said simply. 'That's all.'

'Oh.' No one could accuse him of unnecessary sweet talk.

'I'd like to bet that once you get to know me a little, you'll find I'm quite a reasonable sort of guy,' he continued, so seriously she suspected he was mocking her again. 'You might even like me.'

Surprisingly she wanted to smile but firmly quelled the impulse. If there was one thing Zac Lawson *didn't* need, it was encouragement. 'You're very sure of yourself.'

'And that's something you don't like.' Suddenly there was no amusement under the surface. 'Was he like that?'

'He?' She'd frozen and she saw the cat eyes registering the fact. Careful, she warned herself. Don't let you guard down.

'This guy who let you down so badly,' he said quietly.

She didn't have to ask this time. 'Jennie,' she stated stiffly. She could strangle her. What else had Jennie said?

He didn't deny it. 'She said some guy led you up the garden path, that's all. No details except you're well rid of him.'

That said it all really. 'It's past history,' she said briefly, hoping he would take the hint. 'Finished with.'

He surveyed her for a moment more and then, to her

amazement, stretched his long legs, saying lazily, 'They never make these things with enough leg room. For me, that is. Now, this restaurant was personally recommended and I understand they do a terrific 20-ounce steak with pepper sauce, but I'm reserving judgement. The steaks back home are second to none.'

It took her a moment to accept she was off the hook. A little shakily, she murmured, 'I hope they do smaller ones too.'

Again his eyes locked on to hers. 'They will do whatever you require them to do, Rachel.' A glimmer of a smile touched the firm lips. 'I will make sure of it.'

She nodded, turning to look out of the window but without really seeing the brightly lit shop windows and scurrying commuters with their umbrellas. Funnily enough, she had no doubt whatsoever that people would always do what Zac Lawson told them and it was far from reassuring.

CHAPTER THREE

RACHEL had heard about the restaurant Zac had chosen
but had never ventured inside its exalted doors, mainly
because it was the kind of place that didn't print prices
on its menus and didn't stock a bottle of wine under
forty pounds or more. It was still early, only half past
six, but quite a few of the tables were occupied as they
were shown to a secluded alcove where they could see
the whole dining area but remain private. She was vitally
conscious of the other customers and extremely thankful she'd decided to wear her new and expensive suit
today and bring out her Gucci shoes and bag—mainly
to instil confidence when facing Jeff. As it was, he had
been somewhat sheepish, clearly regretting his outburst
the day before and listening to her explanation about the
sales team without interrupting.

'Fancy a cocktail while we look at the menu?' At
her nod Zac raised his hand and a waiter appeared like
a genie out of a bottle. She listened to him order two
champagne cocktails and then returned her gaze to the
enormous embossed menu the waiter had placed in her
hand after she'd been seated.

The menu was printed in several different languages
but the words blurred as her head swam. It was hard
to take in that she was sitting in these sumptuous

surroundings with Zac Lawson. She hadn't known he existed twenty-four hours ago, but from the moment she'd met him he'd invaded her thoughts whether she was awake or asleep. Which was difficult to come to terms with.

She took a deep breath as the cocktail waiter reappeared, thanking him as he placed a champagne flute in front of her. Zac held out his own glass so she was forced to do the same, and as they touched, he murmured, 'To a pleasant evening.' And then he smiled, adding meekly, 'Is that acceptable?'

She couldn't help smiling back. 'I guess.'

'At last,' he said, very softly.

'Sorry?' She stared at him, puzzled.

'I've been waiting for that first real smile.' He tilted his head slightly as he studied her. 'I wasn't wrong.'

Was he going to be this enigmatic all night? 'Wrong?'

'I knew your smile would light up your face.'

That was *so* something Giles would have come out with. She knew her face had stiffened but she couldn't do anything about it. Charming, and delivered in such a way it didn't sound cheesy.

'Whoops, I take it I've made another mistake. You're a woman who doesn't like compliments,' he said quietly.

Rachel stared at him for a moment as she tried to formulate a reply. 'I like them if they're genuine,' she said at last, and she didn't care that it sounded rude.

'And you think I wasn't being genuine?' he said thoughtfully. 'Interesting. Very interesting.'

Had he taken lessons in being aggravating? She lifted her chin, determined not to ask him what he meant this time, and took a sip of her cocktail. It was delicious.

She'd had what had passed for a champagne cocktail before but it hadn't tasted anything like as good. This was in a league all of its own.

Zac's gaze had returned to his menu and after another sip she put her glass down and focused on the choice of food. By the time the ever-attentive waiter, who'd been hovering nearby, glided to the table she was able to order the smoked salmon and bean salad, followed by grilled chicken with honey-glazed figs in a manner that declared she was perfectly in control.

'No steak?' Zac asked softly.

'No, I prefer chicken.' Ridiculous, because she would probably have had a small steak but for him suggesting it earlier. She shook her head mentally at herself, marvelling that there was a whole side to her personality she hadn't known about, and a side she wasn't particularly proud of. She had to get a grip.

Zac ordered the smoked salmon too, followed by his 20-ounce steak, along with a bottle of wine from the wine waiter, and then settled back in his seat, a faint gleam in his eyes. It wasn't a gleam that inspired confidence and Rachel knew she'd been right to be wary when he said, 'Are you always so prickly?'

'Prickly? I'm not prickly,' she said immediately.

'Defensive, then. Wary. Call it what you will.'

'I'm not—' She stopped abruptly. She was so tense, her muscles ached. Something had to give, and considering he really hadn't done anything wrong it was her. She forced her vocal cords to form coherent words. 'I'm sorry,' she said carefully, 'I don't mean to be. This hasn't been the greatest year and perhaps I just need the Christmas break more than I knew.'

His eyes roamed over her face for a moment, and when he spoke there was no amusement in his smoky voice. 'I'm sorry too,' he said very quietly, 'that it hasn't been a good year for you. Do you want to talk about it?'

She shrugged in what she hoped was a casual way. 'I got involved with someone who wasn't what he seemed, to put it mildly. A couple of days after he proposed, his wife came to see me.' She pulled a face. 'Big surprise.'

'You didn't know he was married?' He'd sat up straighter.

'Of course not,' she said, shocked.

He nodded. 'No, of course not,' he murmured, almost to himself. 'How long had you been seeing him?'

'A few months.' She didn't want to do this. 'Still, lucky escape,' she said with forced lightness. 'At least I was able to walk away without any messy complications, unlike his wife.' She turned her head, glancing round the discreetly lit room. 'This is a lovely place. If the food is as good as the decor, it will be wonderful.'

The rain was beating against the windows of the restaurant but in the womb-like surroundings all was soft music and muted conversation, the glass chandeliers overhead, fine linen tablecloths and gleaming silver cutlery and crystal creating an aura of cosseted comfort. Another world.

This time he didn't allow her to change the conversation so easily. Quietly, he said, 'Do you still care for him?'

She brushed her hair off her shoulder and looked straight into his eyes. 'No, not in the least. Within weeks I was quite clear about that, if nothing else. I just couldn't...' She paused, amazed her tongue had run away with her.

'What?' He leaned forward in his seat, his eyes narrowed.

She swallowed. 'I couldn't believe I could be with someone for so long and not suspect anything, not realize it was all false, make-believe. Giles was so plausible, so...' She shook her head. 'Big learning curve,' she said brightly. 'And what about you? Is there someone back in Canada? Someone special?'

Calm golden eyes held her. 'No,' he said.

Rachel reached for her champagne flute and finished the rest of her cocktail. It had been a big mistake to come here with Zac tonight. He was too...Her brain failed to come up with a definition and she set her glass down carefully. Too everything. 'So what's the business that's brought you over to England?' she asked, when the silence became uncomfortable. 'If it's not confidential, of course.'

He'd relaxed back in his seat once more and now he smiled. 'It's part business, part pleasure, to be truthful.'

She felt a frisson of something she couldn't name at the word 'pleasure' and hoped desperately the golden eyes hadn't noticed anything. This really was ridiculous.

'I'm here to liaise with a large manufacturing group about an advance in new technology—pick their brains, if you will. My father is aware the world is changing fast and the glass industry constantly needs to change with it. He's something of a visionary, if the truth be known, but he's rarely wrong. And I liked the idea of coming back to the old country and seeing again where I was born, looking up the old haunts and family too, of course. I haven't had a holiday for years, so I don't feel too guilty.'

She returned his smile, hers just a bit shaky, and as the waiter placed their first courses in front of them, she was glad of something to do with her hands. She didn't want to get to know Zac Lawson, she thought, panic-stricken. It was much too dangerous. He was the type of man it was far better to keep at a safe distance. Like at the other side of the world.

She took her first bite of the smoked salmon and bean salad. The thin strips of fish, cooked beans and salad were enhanced by a mustard dressing and dusting of mozzarella, and her taste buds exploded. 'This is gorgeous.' She raised her eyes to see Zac studying her. 'Absolutely gorgeous.'

'Just what I was thinking,' he murmured softly.

Again, it ought to have sounded cheesy but it didn't, which was more scary than anything else. She took another bite of smoked salmon and wondered again how she had got herself into this mess. Act naturally, she told herself firmly. One of your strengths is being a good communicator, so communicate. Raising her head, she said brightly, 'I take it you're intending to be home in time for Christmas? Your business will be finished by then?'

'Sure thing. Christmas is a time for being where the heart is.' The tawny eyes crinkled at the corners as he smiled.

Nice sentiment—if you knew where your heart was. Oh, stop the cynicism! she thought irritably. 'It sounds like you're close to your parents. Any siblings?'

'Nope, just me. They wanted more but it didn't happen and they chose not to go down the medical route. I spent lots of time at Jennie's house during my childhood, though, so I didn't miss out or get spoilt. What about you? Having two sisters must have been fun. Do you see much of them now you're in London?'

'Not a lot,' she said carefully. 'My sisters are near in age so they've always tended to be a closed unit, more like twins really. They're married now and live a few doors from each other.'

He nodded. 'What about your parents?'

'My father died when I was little more than a baby, I don't remember him at all. My mother…' She hesitated. 'She opened a flower shop after my father's death and has always worked hard to make it a success, so I didn't see too much of her. My grandma more or less brought the three of us up, but she died a few years ago after a short illness.'

'And you miss her,' he said softly, his eyes intent on her face.

Oh, yes. She dreaded to think of the adult she might have become but for her grandmother. For every negative spoken about her by her mother, her grandma had spoken a loving positive. In the same way she'd always known her mother didn't like her very much, she'd known she was her grandmother's favourite and it had been balm to a little girl's bruised heart. 'Yes, I miss her,' she said quietly. More than words could express.

Since her grandmother's death just before she had left university and she and Jennie and Susan had come to London, she had stopped returning home to Kent for Christmas. There had been no point. Her sisters were wrapped up in their own lives and virtual strangers to her now, and in previous years her mother had spent every Christmas re-emphasising in word and deed what a failure she considered her youngest daughter. Without her beloved grandmother as a buffer, home would have been unendurable.

From the first, she had maintained she was perfectly happy to stay at the flat and enjoy a quiet Christmas, but her friends wouldn't hear of it. Jennie and Susan had taken it in turns to invite her to their respective homes, and as both girls came from large friendly families the Christmas break had turned into something to look forward to rather than dread. Strangely, though, she found she missed her grandmother more at Christmas time than any other. Or perhaps it wasn't so strange.

Zac brought her attention back to himself when he said, 'Christmas in my home town is always a big deal. Snow, carols, church on Christmas Day, followed by too big a lunch so we have to walk the dogs for hours in the afternoon to work up an appetite for high tea.' His voice was easy, relaxed, but she was aware his gaze was tight on her face.

Rachel got the feeling he was talking to give her time to compose herself, and she found she needed it. Taking a deep breath, she said, 'Snow guaranteed, I suppose? It's very hit and miss here in the south of England. Susan lives near Scotland, though, and last year it was Christmas-card stuff. We even went on a horse-drawn sleigh ride.'

'You spent Christmas with Susan's family last year? You didn't go home?'

Rachel bit her lip. She might have known he would pick up on it. Zac didn't miss a thing. 'No, I didn't go home.'

He made no further comment, instead taking the conversation into less personal paths. They had covered politics, music, books and even the current economic climate by the time dessert—roasted peaches with butterscotch—was finished.

And gradually Rachel found she'd relaxed, mainly

because it was impossible not to with Zac. He was a fascinating and congenial dinner companion with a slightly wicked sense of humour, which was often directed against himself. She might have found this endearing but for the fact Giles had done the same thing, a charming ploy to hook the latest fish in Giles's case. As for Zac? Who knew?

Not that it mattered, she told herself, laughing at something he'd said. She wasn't involved with this man, unlike Giles, and didn't have to concern herself with whether he was the genuine article or not. After the champagne cocktail and two glasses of excellent wine, followed by a liqueur with her coffee, she'd come to the decision she had got into the habit of taking herself and the world in general too seriously. She was in fabulous surroundings with a drop-dead-gorgeous man on an evening out that definitely wouldn't be repeated—she was determined about that even if he asked for another date, which she doubted—and she should live for the moment.

And to be honest, she admitted to herself as she popped one of the to-die-for hand-made chocolates they'd brought with the coffee into her mouth, there was something very nice in being the recipient of so many envious female glances during the evening. Especially after the knock her ego had taken in the last months. Every woman who'd caught sight of Zac had done a double take. While that might become annoying in time, for a one-off like this evening it made her feel like the cat with the cream. It had been months since she'd felt as light-hearted as she did right now, months since she'd laughed without having to force the sound. Whether it was an act or not, Zac was very good at what he did. She had to give him that.

When Zac ordered more liqueurs and coffee Rachel
didn't object, even though she realised with a little jolt
of surprise it was nearly ten o'clock. The time had flown
by, and when eventually Zac called the waiter over and
settled the bill, she glanced at her watch and saw another
hour had passed. Zac stood up and pulled out her chair
for her, taking her arm as they walked out of the restaurant into the huge foyer beyond. When he helped her
on with her coat, his tall muscular physique seemed to
dwarf everybody around him, and the attractive blonde
receptionist couldn't take her eyes off him, not that Zac
appeared to notice. She didn't doubt he had, though.

It was cold outside but the rain clouds had blown
away and the sky was high and pierced with stars. The
fresh night air made her realise she was feeling the ef-
fects of the wine and liqueurs, and she told herself she
needed to keep her wits about her. She suddenly felt
uncomfortably vulnerable.

The taxi Zac had ordered when he'd paid the bill
was waiting at the kerb. He took her arm again as he
helped her into the car and although it was nothing but
a polite gesture, the pressure of his hand on her body
made her cheeks flush. Zac had taken her briefcase
from the cloakroom attendant and as he slung it onto
his side of the seat she wished it was between them. As
it was, a hard male thigh rested against hers and his
arm stretched along the top of the seat behind her. She
wondered if he would try for a goodnight kiss and her
heart thumped.

'I'm sorry I've kept you so late. Will you be up to the
early hours?' he asked softly, glancing down at her.

She tried to relax her fingers, which were clenched
together in her lap. 'I'm sorry?' she said, having only
half heard him.

'You said you had work to do,' he reminded her.

She had. Amazingly she'd forgotten. Jeff had asked her to go over the failed project with a fine-toothed comb and detail the sales team's part in the disaster for a report he had to submit to the managing director by the end of the week. 'What I have to do will take a while.' And a clear head. Plenty of black coffee when she got in. 'We lost a lucrative contract due to certain folk refusing to pull their weight, and my boss needs the facts and figures for his boss.'

He raised his brows. 'So you really do have to work?'

'I told you,' she said reprovingly.

He nodded. 'So you did, but I suspected it was an excuse not to have dinner with me.'

'Well, I might have said the same anyway but tonight it does happen to be true.'

He gave a roar of a laugh that brought a smile to her lips. 'And was the ordeal so terrible?' he asked wryly.

'The meal was very nice,' she said primly. 'Thank you.'

'And the company?' he persisted. 'Was that very nice too?'

'Tolerable.' But she smiled again to soften the word. She *had* enjoyed herself despite all expectations, and it had been seductively gratifying to be sought out by a man like Zac.

The edges of his mouth curved up. 'Tolerable enough to be repeated?'

Her heart had just about settled into its normal pattern; now it pounded like a sledgehammer again. She shook her head quickly. 'I'm sorry, I can't. But thank you.'

'Yes, you can. You just say, "Thank you, Zac. That would be great," and the job's done. Simple.'

Nothing was simple with Zac Lawson. And with him so close and the scent and warmth of him enfolding her, it was getting more complicated by the second. Rachel took a deep breath. This had to be nipped in the bud, right now. 'What I mean is—'

'I know what you mean, Rachel,' he said, his voice holding only the faintest trace of amusement. 'Believe me, you're nothing if not crystal clear. And Jennie told me you don't date so there's no misunderstanding on that score. I'd just like you to share a meal with me now and again while I'm over here, that's all. Business in the day and hotel rooms at night are OK, but eating alone can get pretty tedious.'

She stared into the dark face lit now and again by the lights flashing by outside the taxi windows. His voice had been casual, deceptively so. For a moment she almost believed him if it wasn't for those unusual tawny eyes so intent on her face. Jennie had told him she didn't date and for a man like Giles—or in this case, Zac—such a challenge couldn't be ignored. Keeping her voice even and steady, she said calmly, 'You mean as a friend? Dinner companions?'

'Exactly.' He nodded. 'Friends.'

'Purely platonic.' She raised one eyebrow.

'Right.' He nodded again. 'Sure thing.'

Yeah, and pigs could fly. 'But I'm sure there'll be lots of business colleagues willing to have dinner with you.' And all of them women. 'And Jennie's free most nights, Susan too. You could meet her Henry, he's a lovely man.'

'I'm sure he is,' he said, his Canadian burr warm. 'But I enjoy *your* company and I had a good time tonight.'

So had she. That was the trouble.

'And the thing is, we know where we stand with each other, right?' he added, shifting slightly in his seat.

'I'm sorry?' She couldn't think with him so close.

He assumed a patient tone. 'I'm over here for a short time so there's no question of any romantic attachments, and some women—even after one date—can make things a little awkward.'

Now, she did believe that. She bet women tried to stick to him like limpets; she might have done before Giles had woken her up to the fact that such men were dangerous.

'You're not looking for togetherness or anything permanent at the moment, so what's the harm in us enjoying each other's company for a couple of weeks, no strings attached?'

'As friends?' she emphasised again.

'Sure. That's not to say I don't think you're kind of nice, pretty too. And under that outward facade you're soft and funny and sweet.'

Yeah, yeah, yeah. 'There's one thing I'm not, Zac,' she said, a touch of steel in her voice. 'And that's willing in the bed department.' She stared straight at him and she wasn't smiling.

His languid gaze stroked over her face. He grinned. 'You think I'm a wolf?' he drawled lazily. 'Of the big bad variety?'

'Aren't you?' she prevaricated.

'Not these days.' Something flashed in the golden eyes and was gone. 'Although I won't say I'd be able to resist doing this occasionally.'

His lips had taken hers before she could do anything about it. It was a confident kiss, firm and sexy, his mouth exploring hers with an expertise that was far from chaste.

Rachel knew she'd stiffened but the sensual stirring of her blood and the knowledge that she'd wondered all night what this would be like kept her from pulling away. And all her imaginings couldn't have prepared her for the impact anyway.

He broke the kiss before she regained enough control to finish it, lifting his head and smoothing the outline of her lips with the pad of his thumb. 'Just a kiss,' he said very softly, 'because I'm not a wolf, Rachel. OK?'

She hoped he couldn't feel she was shaking. It was the hardest thing she'd ever done, to pull herself together and speak coherently. 'You prove you're not a wolf by kissing me?' she asked, proud of the slightly amused note she managed to inject into her tone and hiding her trembling hands in her lap.

'Absolutely,' he said firmly. 'A wolf wouldn't have stopped at a kiss, he'd have pressed his advantage by continuing until he got you to his hotel room which, of course, he would have arranged with the taxi driver beforehand.'

'And you didn't do that.' Good line, she thought cynically.

'I rest my case.' His eyes lingered on the fullness of her lips and her body heat increased tenfold.

Her throat worked around a tight swallow, her mouth tingling from his kiss. She was equally amazed and devastated by her body's reaction. She had thought herself in love with Giles but even in her most abandoned moments he hadn't aroused her like this, and Zac Lawson was virtually a stranger—and a stranger she didn't like at that. No, she corrected herself in the next instant. It wasn't that she didn't like him. Didn't trust or approve of him was more to the point. Which made it even more humiliating, if anything. She just hoped and prayed he didn't know.

'Have I convinced you?'

She'd been so lost in the maelstrom of her thoughts that she blinked before she said, 'That you're not a wolf? Hardly. Apart from the fact that I think this reasoning is flawed, it could be a clever tactic on your part.'

He considered that for a moment. 'Then the only way you can prove if I'm genuine is to see me again.' He smiled winningly. 'The proof of the pudding is in the eating.'

She opened her mouth to tell him that she was not—absolutely, one hundred per cent *not*—going to see him again and looked into the liquid gold of his eyes. Last week, and all the weeks before it after she'd finished with Giles, had been the same. Work, the odd evening out with the girls, nights when she'd washed her hair and done her nails or watched the latest DVD with Jennie or Susan if they'd been in. Her choice, admittedly. She'd been asked out by men on several occasions but had politely declined. And it wasn't that Zac had persisted, not really. From the moment she'd seen him there had been sparks of electricity in the air.

It was a relief to admit it at last.

'So,' he drawled lazily as the taxi drew into the mews. 'How about putting me to the test tomorrow night? Dinner again?'

'Tomorrow?' Rachel discovered it was possible to feel flattered and harassed at the same time.

His smile deepened. 'Why not?'

She gave him a long, silent look as the taxi pulled to a halt outside her door. 'You don't give up easily, do you?'

He opened the car door and exited the vehicle, helping

her out and then pulling her into the circle of his arms as he said, 'I never give up. The words don't feature in my psyche.'

A red light was flashing bright and strong in the back of her mind but she was dealing with the sensations caused by being in his arms and couldn't cope with anything else. She waited for the kiss she was sure was coming and felt disappointment out of all proportion when he gently guided her to the doorstep and dropped a light kiss on her nose.

'Goodnight, Rachel,' he said softly. 'Sweet dreams.'

It was on the tip of her tongue to remind him she wouldn't get a lot of sleep that night, that she was going to be working half of it as it was. But somehow she found she didn't want to spoil the moment. Instead, she took her briefcase from him and watched him walk back to the taxi.

He paused with his hand on the door, turning to look back at her as she stood motionless in the shadows. 'I'll pick you up at eight tomorrow—that'll give you time to get home and change into something less formal,' he said quietly. 'I thought we'd go somewhere to eat that has a dance floor.'

Hang on a minute, that was too much like a proper date. Rachel opened her mouth to protest but he'd slid into the taxi on the last words, shutting the door firmly behind him. The next moment the vehicle had drawn away.

She stood for some moments staring after the taxi, even when it had disappeared. She was going to regret this. Something deep inside told her dealing with Giles had been a piece of cake compared to coping with Zac

Lawson. So why had she agreed to have dinner with him again tomorrow?

The answer did nothing to reassure her. Because every fibre of her being wanted to.

CHAPTER FOUR

WHEN her alarm woke her the next morning after only three hours' sleep, Rachel glanced across the room to where Jennie was snuggled under the covers of her own bed. As she did so, her friend groaned the words she used every morning. 'It can't be time to get up yet.'

''Fraid so.' She was dreading facing Jennie this morning. When she'd entered the house last night both Jennie and Susan had gone to bed, and at four in the morning, when she'd finally finished the report to her satisfaction and crept into the room she shared with Jennie, her friend hadn't woken. She had been so tired she'd fallen asleep as soon as her head touched the pillow, but now she was awake, the worry that had troubled her last night and made the report even more difficult to formulate was at the forefront of her mind.

As Jennie sat up in bed, pushing her mass of shining black hair out of her eyes, Rachel said quickly, 'Jen, I'm sorry about Zac. I didn't expect or look for it, I promise you.'

'What?' Jennie yawned sleepily. 'Oh, Zac. Hey, it's not your fault if he fancies you rather than me. Did you have a nice time?' she added on another jaw-breaking yawn.

This was making her feel worse. 'It was OK,' she

said warily. 'The meal was nice and the restaurant was fabulous.'

'Seeing him again?' Jennie swung her feet out of bed, standing and stretching before padding over to Rachel's bed and plumping down at the end of it. 'He's too yummy not to, surely?'

'Uh-huh. Tonight, actually. He—he doesn't like eating alone,' she finished lamely. 'That's all there is to it.'

Jennie sat up straighter. 'Tonight? He's a fast worker, I'll give him that. Must be in the family genes.' She giggled.

'Jen, I really am sorry, I mean that.'

'Don't be.' Jennie became serious all at once. 'Susan and I were saying last night it's about time you got into the stream again and the perfect person to get your feet wet with is Zac. He can wine and dine you and you can have fun without worrying that it's going to get heavy with him only being around for three weeks. Just enjoy yourself, Cinders. Heaven knows, you deserve a break after Rat Face.' Rat Face was her friends' name for Giles. 'Anyway, to be perfectly honest, if Zac had fancied me it would have been a complication. There's a guy from one of the fashion houses who's asked me out and he's gorgeous, I've had my eye on him for a while.'

Rachel knew Jennie was telling the truth; if nothing else, her friend was transparently honest. Feeling better, she said, 'What's he like?' knowing such a prompt would keep Jennie going all through breakfast, thereby deflecting any question about her evening with Zac. For some reason she didn't want to talk about it, not even to Jennie and Susan, possibly because she didn't know how she felt. Or maybe because she did.

The strategy worked, and by the time the three women left the flat Rachel's mind was at rest about Jennie. Susan had asked casually if she'd had a nice time the night before but that was all, and even when Jennie had finished waxing lyrical about the amazing Keir, the conversation hadn't turned to Zac.

Rachel turned and looked after her two friends, whose work places were in the opposite direction from hers. Come to think of it, she thought with a frown, they had both shown a remarkable lack of nosiness, which was totally uncharacteristic and could only mean they'd agreed to tread softly-softly. Which was nice of them—in a way—but made her feel slightly exasperated too because she didn't need to be treated with kid gloves as though she was some kind of victim. Mind you, she wouldn't have wanted to talk about Zac if they *had* asked...

Deciding she was in danger of becoming as nutty as a fruit cake, she walked swiftly on, turning her mind to the papers she had worked on half the night and resolutely putting all thoughts of Zac Lawson out of her head. Nevertheless, she had decided that tonight would be the last time she would agree to see him. In the cold light of day she knew it would be madness to do anything else.

Rachel was putting the finishing touches to her make-up when Zac arrived at the flat that evening. She heard Jennie or Susan let him in and then the sound of voices and laughter from the sitting room. She felt an instant tightening in her stomach in response to his deep chuckle. Shutting her eyes tightly for a moment, she then opened them slowly on a long intake of breath and stared at the girl in the mirror.

Anxious eyes looked back at her and she clicked her tongue in annoyance at the expression on her face. For goodness' sake, she could do better than this. She had all the sexiness of a scared rabbit at the moment. Inhaling again, she relaxed her taut facial muscles and tried a smile. Better. Not brilliant, but better.

Her eyes ran over her reflection from the top of her head to her vertiginous high heels. She'd spent some time putting her hair up and now it curled in smooth coils at the back of her head, the few strands she'd left down to soften the style catching the light and gleaming like strands of copper. Her silk-jersey dress was a deep cornflower blue and highlighted the blue of her eyes, its plunging neckline showing her newly regained curves to their full advantage.

Compared to some of the daring frocks Jennie favoured, her dress was fairly circumspect, but Rachel knew it suited her and she needed every ounce of confidence she could summon up tonight. She swallowed hard. On impulse she reached for a sexy red lipstick she'd bought a few weeks ago in a moment of madness but had never worn, favouring discreet pinks and peaches normally. Once applied, she was amazed how something so simple as a lipstick could alter her whole persona. Suddenly she felt flirtatious, even a little wanton, and it was heady.

Reason asserted itself and she frowned. This evening wasn't about being provocative, just the opposite, in fact. Her hand reached for a tissue to wipe her lips but in the same moment Jennie opened the bedroom door and sailed in, her eyes bright. 'He's waiting and he looks like a million dollars,' she said in a loud whisper. 'You're going to be the envy of every woman on the planet tonight. Come *on*.' She pulled Rachel towards the door,

thrusting the satin cocktail purse in the exact shade of
the dress into one hand. 'Zac's got a taxi waiting. You
look absolutely sensational, by the way.'

Sensational was stretching it a bit, but Rachel saw
Jennie hadn't exaggerated about Zac. He looked wickedly sexy and extremely dangerous, a supreme Casanova
in every sense of the word. Somehow she managed to
return his smile and disguise the bolt of lightning that
had shot through her as she'd taken in the hard male
body encased in a dark charcoal suit cut impeccably to
flaunt broad, muscled shoulders and strong thighs—or it
seemed to her he was flaunting them anyway. Whatever,
he was sex on legs and for the first time in her life she
actually felt weak at the knees. Wishing she had Jennie's
experience to cope with a man like Zac, she adopted
what she hoped came over as an easy, casual attitude
as she said, 'Sorry to have kept you waiting.'

'You didn't, I was early.' He stepped forward and
brushed her cheek with his lips. He smelled delicious.
'And even if I'd waited hours it would have been worth
it. You look beautiful.'

She was vitally aware of Jennie and Susan hovering
in the background, their faces alight, and felt hotly embarrassed without really knowing why. Wanting nothing
more now than to be on their way, she took refuge in
what Jennie had said, 'The taxi must be costing you a
fortune. We'd better go, hadn't we?'

He didn't reply, merely helping her into her coat and
taking her arm as they left. Outside, the December night
reflected the change in the weather over the last twenty-
four hours. Rain and heavy clouds had given way to
a clear sky and icy-dry cold, the first real frost of the
winter scattering the small mews with diamond dust.
Rachel didn't feel the chill, though. Zac's body against

hers was sending the blood rushing through her veins like wildfire. Her own personal central heating.

Once in the warmer confines of the taxi cab, she settled into a corner of the seat but Zac was having none of it. He slid an arm round her shoulders, moving her closer against him as he asked casually, 'So how did you get on with that report or whatever it was you had to present today?'

Trying to match his nonchalant attitude and ignore the mad fluttering in her stomach, she crossed her legs and simulated a calm she didn't feel. 'Fine, thank you. There were no problems.'

'And your boss's boss was satisfied?'

'As far as I know. He hasn't complained yet anyway.'

'Good. Did I tell you how beautiful you look, by the way?'

'Yes, you did. A minute or so ago.'

When in the next moment she felt him gently nuzzle her upswept hair, Rachel sat as stiff as a board, willing herself not to shiver. She was *not* going to play his flirting game, no way.

'Your hair smells of apples,' he said softly.

She was wearing an exotic perfume, the cost of which had been a week's salary, and Zac liked the scent of her cheap supermarket brand shampoo? 'It obviously does what it says on the bottle, then,' she returned lightly. 'The shampoo's called Apple Blossom.'

'Nice,' he murmured smokily, the hand over her shoulder idly playing with one of the strands of hair she'd left loose.

A quiet heat began to creep through her body, which was all the prompting she needed to break the intimate mood that had fallen. Shifting infinitesimally away from him on the pretext of turning to face him, she said, 'And how did your day pan out?'

'Good.' If he noticed her manoeuvre he didn't comment on it, but now his hand rested on the back of the seat behind her. 'Real good. One of the guys invited me down to his weekend place in the country; he and his wife escape London most weekends apparently and take in country pursuits, horseriding and fishing and the rest of it by day and dinner parties by night. Open house apparently. He suggested I might like to bring a partner.'

For a second or two her brain refused to function and then the thought process clicked on through the shock. Jennie had been more right that she'd known when she'd called her cousin a fast worker. 'You're asking me to go away with you for the weekend?' she said weakly. After *one* dinner? Damn cheek.

'I'm asking you to accompany me to a country house as a friend, no strings attached,' he returned gravely. 'Separate bedrooms and all that, of course. Everything above board.'

Yes, it darned well would be—if she agreed to go. Which she wouldn't, of course. 'I'm busy this weekend.'

'Doing what?' he asked bluntly.

Typical, she thought. Any other man would politely express regret and leave it at that, but not Zac Lawson. 'Various things.' She hoped she sounded nonchalant rather than jittery.

'Things on a level like attending a conference on world peace or climate control, or things like washing your hair and having a manicure?' He grinned at her, one eyebrow raised.

Suddenly she wanted to smile but she controlled the

impulse. He didn't need any encouragement. 'Zac, I have a life,' she said sternly. 'Commitments, arrangements, appointments.'

'So it's the washing-your-hair scenario?' His voice was still relaxed, easy, but his eyes never left her face.

She frowned. 'I don't have to explain what I'm doing to you.'

He bent his head and kissed her. Nothing touched but their mouths, but at the end of it Rachel's shaky composure had crumbled, her breathing disjointed and a warm sweet ache spread through her body. Her eyes had shut of their own volition and when she dazedly opened them after his mouth had lifted she was almost surprised to find herself in the real world, the lights flashing by outside the window of the cab making her blink.

'I'm only here for a while,' Zac said throatily, 'and it would be nice to spend my spare time with you. Say you'll come.'

It was crazy, madness, and there were a million reasons to say no, to cut this ridiculous liaison right now, but breathing in the scented warmth of him and looking into the glittering tawny eyes, her mind stubbornly refused to come up with one. Her cheeks were burning and she knew she was trembling. She just hoped he didn't know too. 'I—I'll think about it,' she heard herself say as another part of her mind protested, No, no, no; wrong answer.

'That'll do for now.' His gaze unlocked from hers and as he settled back in his seat, his arm once again loosely round her shoulders, Rachel tried to regulate her breathing.

The nightclub was plush and the meal and wine were excellent, the small parquet dance floor full of couples dancing to the live music most of the time. After that one blistering kiss in the taxi, Zac had metamorphosed into a genial and amusing dinner companion and more than once he had made her laugh until she had cried. As the level in the bottle of wine had diminished, Rachel had found it easier to relax. Zac had put himself out to be non-threatening and it was comfortable to go with the flow. Her fragile aplomb faltered a little when he asked her to dance between the second and third courses, but the band was playing a lively number and apart from his hand on her arm to and from the dance floor, they barely touched.

When she made a visit to the ladies cloakroom—a vision in chrome and satin with wall-to-wall full-length mirrors in the outer section—she had to acknowledge she was enjoying herself. Very much. Definitely too much, if she thought about it. But she wasn't going to think about it, she determined, fiddling with her hair before applying more lipstick. As Zac had said, he was here for a short time and then gone. End of story. And as she had no intention of sleeping with him and had made that very clear, she had nothing to worry about.

She returned to the table to find her pudding—a seriously delicious red wine syllabub with blueberries—waiting for her, along with a glass of honey-sweet dessert wine. Reflecting that it was *so* nice to be wined and dined and cosseted, she downed the wine with reckless abandon and ate every scrap of the syllabub. It was then that Zac leant forward, his golden eyes soft and glowing in the muted lighting and his firm, faintly stern mouth smiling. 'So,' he murmured. 'Made a decision on the weekend yet?'

CHAPTER FIVE

'You're doing what?' Jennie squealed, she and Susan staring at Rachel, their breakfast forgotten. 'Did I hear right?'

'I'm going to a house party in the country with Zac for the weekend,' Rachel repeated, knowing she'd gone as red as a beetroot. 'It's nothing heavy. A business colleague took pity on him, being away from home and all that, and Zac invited me along as a friend. He's picking me up here after work and we're driving down to somewhere near Guildford.'

'Right.' Susan recovered first. 'Sounds great. It's just that things seem to be moving fast and it's not like you.'

None of this was like her, Rachel reflected miserably. In the cold light of day she was having second thoughts, but the deed was done. She'd agreed to spend the weekend with him and that was that. 'Things *aren't* moving in the way you mean,' she insisted quietly. 'I told you, I'm going as a friend, that's all.'

'Right,' Susan said again, but Jennie was less diplomatic.

'A friend?' she hooted. 'Cinders, a girl's *friends* with geek types or gay men or happily married guys, none of which Zac is. What are the sleeping arrangements?'

she added. 'Are you sharing a room? I bet you are, aren't you?'

Rachel shook her head. 'Absolutely not. I checked.'

'Sure?' Jennie surveyed her disbelievingly.

'I *told* you.'

'All right, all right.' Jennie held up her hands before reaching for her toast. 'But take your chastity belt just in case, that's all I'm saying.' She rolled her eyes expressively.

Rachel laughed, she couldn't help it. 'No need for that, you know me.'

'Ah, but do you know Zac? Or more to the point, do you know yourself around Zac? One thing's for sure, Cinders, he's not your normal run-of-the-mill male. I've met a few guys with that extra wow factor but Zac's in a league of his own. Funny to think I tagged after him and my brothers as a child, isn't it? He can remember I was a bit of a tomboy and never wanted to play with the girls.'

Susan snorted. 'I find nothing surprising about that. I bet you flirted with the doctor who delivered you.'

Jennie smiled happily. 'Probably. I just *like* men.'

And men liked Jennie, in spite of the way she treated them. Or was it *because* of it? Rachel thought with a little sigh. Whatever, she wished just a smidgen of Jennie's disposition could brush off on her. It would make life so much easier.

She thought the same thing at various intervals throughout the day, her stress level ratcheting up minute by minute as she considered the next forty-eight hours. How could you view something as daunting and thrilling at the same time? Be wildly excited with anticipation one moment and thinking up ways to get out of it the next?

When she realised she'd read an item of correspondence three times and still not taken it in, she pulled herself together. Glancing at her watch, she saw she had a couple of hours left before leaving work and she needed to put her full mind to what she was doing. She'd virtually wasted the day as it was.

When she left the brightly lit, centrally heated confines of the office building, the air was so cold it made her gasp. The weather forecast had predicted a particularly icy spell but after a poor damp summer and even damper autumn Rachel didn't mind the cold. She breathed in long and deeply, relishing the bite of the frosty air and the way it cancelled out the smell of traffic fumes and other city odours. Everyone was bemoaning the fact that the experts were saying it was going to be a hard winter this year, but after several mild ones she felt some icy weather would kill off all the bugs and cleanse the struggling environment. And Christmas was better when it was cold somehow.

Rachel wrinkled her nose at herself as she began to walk. How she'd feel if the worse happened and she had to trudge to work through inches of snow for weeks on end she didn't know, but snow was so pretty, magical in its way.

She endeavoured to keep her mind off the imminent weekend by striding out and concentrating on a brisk walk home, but her stomach was host to a legion of butterflies. Jennie's nonchalant words that morning had struck a nerve that had bothered her more than a little. *Did she know herself around Zac?* She didn't have to think about the answer. Until a few days ago she would have sworn on oath that primal, uncontrollable sexual desire was something she would never have to worry about. But she hadn't met Zac then. And if he'd been a fairly normal, nine-to-five guy who had returned her feelings and with whom she could have envisaged some sort of future, she'd be over the moon right now. But he wasn't, and she wasn't.

And she wanted her first time to mean more than just a notch on a Giles-type bedpost.

She stopped dead as the thought hit. She wasn't seriously thinking about sleeping with Zac, was she? Of course she wasn't. That would be emotional suicide and she didn't have a death wish. She'd make sure her bedroom door was locked each night.

A desultory flake of snow drifted in the wind as she began walking again, the cold nipping at her ears and nose. She sighed deeply. Nature was conspiring against her to make this a Christmas-card-perfect weekend. She didn't doubt that by morning every tree and bush would have a fairy-tale coating of snow, the sky would be a clear cerulean blue and the air would be crisp and perfumed with winter. Zac's colleague's weekend place was absolutely bound to have huge log fires, oak beams and twinkly leaded windows and be set in its own magnificent grounds. It was written in the stars, she just knew it.

Was she destined to meet men around Christmastime who would break her heart? Again she stopped, only to continue walking on in the next moment but now giving herself a good talking-to. Giles had *not* broken her heart, although she'd thought he had for a week or two until reason had kicked in. And Zac couldn't because he simply wouldn't get the opportunity. She'd had her fingers burnt by one shallow egomaniac, and once bitten, twice shy. And who needed men anyway? Contrary to what Jennie might say, a girl could still have a fulfilling and happy life without a man in tow. Or this girl could, anyway.

The pep talk continued once she got home and had a quick shower before getting ready. Assuming the mode of dress would be warm casual in the day for outside pursuits and smart for evening, she packed accordingly, and had just closed the lid of the case when Zac knocked on the front door.

Her heart gave an almighty leap and then hammered away in her chest like a mad thing, and she took a few seconds to breathe deeply before walking through to the hall.

'Hi.' He'd taken a step back from the door and was standing on the pavement with his hands thrust in the pockets of his big charcoal overcoat, his black hair dusted with snow and his tawny eyes narrowed. Christmas come early.

Rachel swallowed hard. 'Hi.' *Help!*

'All packed?' He still hadn't smiled.

She nodded, ridiculously flustered. 'I'll just get my things and turn off the lights. I won't be a moment.'

She felt rather than saw the big body relax and then he said softly, 'I wondered if you'd change your mind.'

She swallowed again. 'I said I would come, didn't I?'

'And your word is your bond?'

She didn't hesitate. 'Yes, it is.' The house phone began to ring and she turned, saying over her shoulder, 'Come in a minute while I answer the phone.'

Immediately she picked up the receiver she knew it had been one of her more unwise decisions. Her mother's voice was as cold and clipped as always: 'Is Rachel there?'

'It's me, Mum.' Every muscle had tightened at her mother's tone.

'Rachel? I haven't heard from you in over a month.'

It was on the tip of her tongue to ask why—when her mother phoned Lisa and Claire daily—she always had to be the one to pick up the phone, but conscious of Zac feet away, she said carefully, 'I've been busy, a crisis at work.'

'I see.' The wire fairly froze over. 'So busy you couldn't talk to your own mother? You expect me to believe that?'

Don't react, keep calm. The normal mental drill when dealing with her mother was activated. 'I'm sorry, Mum, but I can't really talk now. I was literally walking out of the door when you phoned,' she said woodenly. 'I'm away for the weekend.'

'Oh, yes?' Her mother's voice was full of disbelief. 'Where are you off to and with whom?'

'I'm going to a weekend house party at Guildford with a friend,' she said stiffly, hating the fact she couldn't handle her mother better. Two seconds of talking to her and she always felt guilty and wretchedly at fault.

'Male or female?' her mother sniffed frostily.

'I'm sorry?'

'I asked you if your *friend*—' her mother's voice was laced with scepticism '—is male or female. Surely that's simple enough to answer, girl?'

Rachel wasn't aware that Zac could hear both ends of the conversation—although her mother's voice had always been as sharp and penetrating as a surgeon's scalpel—until he whisked the receiver out of her hand. 'Male, Mrs Ellington,' he said smoothly, 'and we really do have to leave. Perhaps you would like to ring back next week and have a word with Rachel? Have a good weekend and goodbye for now.'

When he replaced the receiver she was too shocked to do more than stare at him. She couldn't believe he'd just done that.

He raked a hand through his damp hair, the look on his face telling her he expected her wrath to break over his head in a consuming flood. 'I'm sorry,' he said quietly. 'That was out of line and I know it. It's just that Jennie told me a little about your mother and I didn't like hearing you treated like that, added to which I didn't want the weekend spoilt before it began with her upsetting you.'

She looked at him, incredulous, mouth slightly open. It was a moment or two before she recovered sufficiently to speak coherently, and then she said, 'That was incredibly presumptuous, whatever your reasoning. I'm not a child.'

'I know it,' he said again. 'And I am truly sorry.'

'I am more than capable of dealing with my own mother.'

'And any other mother, I'm sure.'

Her blue eyes assessed him warily but he stared back at her so innocently she didn't know what to think. Giles had gone down the ingratiating route with her mother, falling over backwards to butter her up. It was only now, at this very moment, that she realised it had stuck in her craw. Nevertheless, Zac's audacity was unbelievable. 'I can't believe you just did that,' she said icily. 'Even now I can't believe it.'

'Neither can I,' he agreed suitably meek.

This was the perfect excuse to throw a blue fit and ask him to leave. But she didn't want to. She hoped her confusion, her helpless rush of desire and bemusement and a hundred and one other emotions she couldn't have put a name to if she'd tried weren't obvious to him. She felt she was walking on the edge of a precipice every moment she was with him, so why was she torturing herself like this for someone who couldn't be more than a fleeting shadow in her life? It didn't make sense. Nothing did.

And then he drew her into his arms, kissing her long and deeply, and she knew why.

When he released her she was flushed, her hair slightly tousled and her breathing erratic. Feeling seventeen rather than a mature twenty-seven, she smiled shakily. 'Is that your answer to everything? Kiss the girl?'

'Not everything,' he murmured. 'And not every girl.'

She brushed her hair from her hot cheeks, feeling hopelessly inadequate to deal with him. 'I'll get my things.'

Zac nodded, and once she brought her case through from the bedroom he took it from her, placing it at his feet before helping her on with her coat. She steeled herself not to shiver at his touch but it was hard. When he'd kissed her his chin had been nice and smooth, he'd obviously shaved in the last hour or so before coming to pick her up. And the now familiar scent of the aftershave he favoured caused a frisson of desire to snake down her nerve-endings. There was something overwhelmingly sexy in knowing he had shaved for her.

He picked up her case and offered her his free arm. 'Shall we go? It was beginning to snow quite heavily when I drove here so maybe it would be prudent to get under way.'

'You drove?' Ridiculously, she hadn't thought about their mode of transport but she supposed she'd imagined a taxi or something, although a taxi all the way to Guildford would be extremely expensive.

'I hired a car for the weekend. That way, if we want to escape the others and have a couple of hours doing something else, it's no hassle,' he said lightly, opening the front door and ushering her out into the mews as he spoke.

Rachel stopped on the doorstep, staring at the sleek lines of the silver-blue Aston Martin parked a few feet away. Why she hadn't noticed it when she'd opened the door to him earlier she didn't know. Then she caught herself. Why would she notice a car when Zac was in front of her? 'This is *some* hire car,' she said weakly. 'The type James Bond would hire for the weekend.'

He grinned, a wicked little grin that for a moment made him almost boyish. 'Designed to impress you,' he admitted wryly. 'Added to which, I drive one back home so it seemed appropriate, even though it took a while to find one.'

She didn't doubt it. It wasn't exactly your average family saloon. 'It's very nice,' she said primly as they walked across the pavement and he opened the passenger door.

'Isn't it?' he said, deadpan.

For a moment she wished Jennie and Susan were there to enjoy a moment she knew the pair of them would relish. Then she reneged on the idea. Far better they didn't have an audience in view of Jennie's comments that morning.

Big fat flakes of feathery snow were now falling from a laden sky and settling fast, and once Zac had slid into the driving seat—his close proximity in the low sports car causing Rachel problems with her breathing again—

he cleared the windscreen. It certainly wasn't a night to be driving anywhere.

With that in mind, she turned to him. 'Do you think it's wise to try and get there in this weather?'

Their eyes met and held. 'Oh, yes,' he said softly.

It took all her will to look away and inject amusement into her voice when she said, 'Perhaps you'd have been better off hiring a four-by-four. I think we might run into trouble in this.'

'And miss the fun of battling against the elements? I don't think so. I like a challenge, Rachel. But, then, you know that.'

It took Rachel a full five minutes to be able to relax her body once they were under way. She had never felt so aware of another human being in her life. His large, capable hands on the steering-wheel, his hard masculine thighs just inches from hers, his narrowed gaze as he concentrated on the road—everything about him stirred her. And yet she knew so little about him. The real him, she amended silently. All the information he'd related so easily had been about his childhood, his family, his work, but nothing whatsoever about his love life, past or present. He seemed to be on very good terms with his secretary, but that could be just his way. And he had told her there was no one back in Canada when they'd first had dinner together. Did she believe that? Her brow creased. She wanted to, which was a problem in itself. And why would a man who looked like Zac and was rich and successful to boot *not* have a girlfriend? It didn't add up.

'What are you thinking?'

His voice startled her and brought colour to her cheeks. She shrugged. 'I was wondering if my mother will ever speak to me again,' she lied. 'She won't appreciate what you did tonight.'

'From what Jennie told me, it would be no great loss if she didn't,' he said smoothly and—in Rachel's opinion—callously. 'But don't worry, she will. Curiosity will prompt her to call, if nothing else.'

It was insightful and absolutely right where her mother was concerned. Rather than comment on what he'd said, she glanced at his chiselled profile. 'I don't know if I like the idea of Jennie talking so freely about me.'

'She didn't. She merely described your mother in a few succinct words, that's all. Painted a picture, you know?'

Knowing Jennie, she could imagine what they had been. She shifted uncomfortably. Changing the subject again, she said, 'How many people are there going to be at the house this weekend?'

'A good few, I think. Martin's the sort of guy who always combines pleasure with business.' He shrugged. 'But he's nice enough and fairly harmless. Expect buffet breakfasts and elaborate dinners and drinks around the fireplace, that sort of deal. Everyone trying to impress everyone else.'

His voice had held a mordant note and she glanced at him again. 'If you disapprove, why did you accept his invitation?'

The amber eyes touched her face for one moment before his gaze returned to the road through the windscreen. 'Because I wanted to spend a whole weekend with you and getting you away from London like this seemed like a heaven-sent opportunity.'

Taken aback, she continued to stare at him for a few moments before forcing herself to turn away. She didn't know what to say and it was probably better to say nothing in view of the warm pleasure his words had evoked. Charm, she warned herself sternly. This was just Zac employing male charm, something Giles had mastered to perfection. It didn't mean anything, not really. And as long as she kept that at the forefront of her mind, she'd be OK. She had to enjoy this weekend as a brief step out of time, that was the way to handle this. A little light-hearted flirting now and again, the odd kiss or two, nothing heavy or particularly meaningful. She had never felt so captivated by a man before and it was as frightening as it was thrilling, but he was only in the country for a short while and she'd made it clear she wasn't in the running for an affair that involved sleeping with him.

Sleeping with him... The warmth became a heat that sent her blood racing. What would it be like to be made love to by Zac? To spend delicious hours in his arms and to wake up beside him in the morning, replete and sexually fulfilled? You only had to look into his eyes to know he would be a skillful and devastatingly seductive lover—the invisible aura of strong sexual magnetism he projected was all the more powerful for being completely natural. Some men had it and some men didn't, and it was nothing to do with looks or wealth, just an inherent part of certain men's personas.

Zac was concentrating on driving in the thick London traffic, conditions made treacherous with the weather, and consequently Rachel found herself deep in a particularly erotic fantasy before she came back to reality and slammed the lid on her wayward libido. Eternally grateful one's thoughts were one's own, she focused her mind on the road ahead, deciding two pairs of eyes were better than one in a snowstorm.

'It's settling fast, isn't it?' she said after a while. Zac was a very competent driver, but the snow had snarled up the traffic and they had crawled the six miles or so to the A3. At this rate, a journey Zac had told her would take a little over an hour would be a lot longer. They had passed two accidents as it was, along with the odd abandoned car by the side of the road. The snow was already inches thick and coming down with a ferocity that commanded respect.

'Don't worry.' He smiled without looking at her. 'We'll be fine. This is a picnic compared to the blizzards we get at home. It really knows how to snow there.'

Granted, but the Canadian authorities were prepared for the onslaught of winter and acted accordingly. England, as always, hadn't, Rachel thought nervously.

By the time they reached the junction signposted Guildford, Portsmouth, they had travelled twenty miles in an hour and a half, and the sat. nav. was telling them they still had over ten miles to travel before reaching their destination. Zac hadn't spoken for the last fifteen minutes, his whole being focused on travelling in the wake of an impressive Range Rover that bulldozed its way through the snow with consummate ease. When the vehicle turned off into a side road shortly after the junction, Rachel glanced at Zac. The Aston Martin, beautiful as it was, wasn't built to cope with snow-packed roads and deep drifts. They were in trouble, whether he admitted it or not.

As though she had spoken, he said reassuringly, 'It's OK. We're two-thirds of the way there.'

Right. Which meant they still had a whole third to go. All thoughts of she and Zac in bed had long since flown out of the window; for the last half an hour she'd been beset by visions of the Aston Martin trapped under a lorry or upended in a ditch or in a head-on collision. She'd decided the last option would be preferable—with the speed of the few brave vehicles still on the road, they'd be sure to survive.

The car had taken it upon itself to show off in one or two spectacular skids, but now it outdid itself as it glided in slow motion in a graceful arc like an Olympic ice skater. Fortunately there wasn't another car in sight when they ended up half off the road facing the wrong way, tilted at a distinctly odd angle.

Zac swore. Once, but very thoroughly. Rachel was just glad they had actually stopped. She breathed out a long silent sigh of relief. They weren't dead. That had to be a bonus.

'Hell, I'm sorry,' Zac said tersely.

It was the first time she had seen him anything less than completely self-assured, and it was almost worth being stuck in a blizzard to experience. Almost. Wishing lunch had been more than a quick sandwich, she tired to ignore her growling stomach. 'It's not your fault. I'm amazed you got this far.' She glanced out of the window into the whirling whiteness. This particular stretch of road was devoid of the comforting lights of civilisation, unlike most they'd travelled on. She wondered when they'd last passed a house or building—she had been so concentrated on the road ahead she couldn't remember.

Zac answered the thought. 'There was a pub a mile or so back. Do you think you could walk that far in this?'

And the alternative option was? 'Of course.' Ignoring the fact she had foolishly decided to wear her new high-heeled suede boots, which had cost a fortune, she nodded firmly. Anything was better than freezing to death and the way the snow was continuing to fall, that was a real possibility. And then she remembered the walking boots she'd packed, along with her wax jacket she'd bought for Christmas in Scotland last year. 'Is there any way you could get my case out of the boot so I could change into my walking boots?' she asked hopefully.

He inclined his head. 'Sure thing.' He grinned at her. 'You're a game little soul, aren't you? No bemoaning the fact I've got us into this mess.'

She tried to ignore how close he was, how the snow had caused his hair to fall over his forehead in a slight quiff, how the hard planes and angles of his face were thrown into stark prominence in the dim light and how very *masculine* he was. Smiling an easy smile she was proud of in the circumstances, she said brightly, 'No good crying over spilt milk, and it could be a lot worse.'

She remembered those words once she was togged up in her walking boots and jacket and had managed to struggle out of the car, which was easier said than done, the angle it was stuck at. As Zac lifted her out and up to stand beside him, her face was assailed by fierce stinging snowflakes and the wind whipped at any exposed flesh. It was absolutely freezing.

Zac had her suitcase along with his, and once he had locked the car he tucked one case under his arm and held the other, leaving a free arm to wrap round her. She had protested she could manage by herself but once they began walking she was glad of his support, the wind so gusty it made staying upright somewhat perilous. Zac seemed unbothered by the elements, his big body moving forwards like a tank, with Rachel clinging to him, partly shielded by his bulk.

It seemed for ever until they rounded a corner and

the lights of the pub pierced the night. As Rachel peered through the tumbling snowflakes she didn't think she had seen anything so welcoming as those lights.

'Nearly there.' Zac hugged her tighter to him. 'OK?'

She could do no more than nod.

'You're a star.' He bent his head and kissed her. A long kiss. And suddenly she didn't feel as cold.

The White Hart was an old eighteenth-century country inn, warm and snug with oak panelling and ancient beams, open fires and a sympathetic landlady. When Zac pushed open the gnarled front door and they all but fell into the copper and brass interior there was a startled silence for a moment, then the buzz of conversation they'd interrupted resumed and the landlady left her place behind the bar and came forward to greet them.

'I take it you're refugees from the storm?' she said as the snow covering them began to melt on the stone-flagged floor. 'What a night! They said snow but we weren't warned it would be as bad as this. Did you have to abandon your car?'

Zac nodded. 'A mile or so down the road.'

'And you were going somewhere nice?' She eyed their suitcases. 'What a shame. Come over by the fire and get warm anyway, and I'll get you a drink on the house. What'll you have? A brandy to warm you up, dear?' she offered, smiling at Rachel, who smiled back wanly.

Rachel had glanced around the pub. It seemed pretty full. The same thought must have occurred to Zac because he said quietly, 'We were going to stay with friends for the weekend but the weather's put paid to that. Have you got a couple of rooms vacant?'

The plump little woman pursed her lips. 'Oh, dear, normally that'd be no problem but we've a party of walkers staying for the weekend.' She gestured at the throng behind her. 'The only thing I could offer you is what we call the attic room on the second floor—it's reached by a staircase off the first floor landing. I don't normally have any call for it because the ceiling is really low and what with the steep stairs and all...' She eyed Zac's six-foot-two, broad-shouldered figure doubtfully. 'But I always keep it aired just in case, and since we had the roof insulated and the new windows it's as warm as toast up there.'

'We'll take it.' Rachel would have curled up on the stoneflagged floor rather than venture outside again. She could see the remains of meals on some of the tables and now she added hopefully, 'Are you still serving food?'

'Oh, aye, dear. It's only half eight.' The landlady smiled cheerily. 'Why don't I show you the room and then you can come down and have a drink while you look at the menu?'

Suddenly the world was back on its axis.

As they followed the landlady—leaving two puddles where they'd been standing—Zac caught hold of Rachel's arm. 'One room,' he murmured softly. 'Sure you're happy with that?'

'Beggars can't be choosers,' she whispered back as they emerged into a back hall, which had a staircase leading from it. 'And it's just somewhere to sleep for tonight.' She met his gaze, adding firmly, 'Just sleep.'

'Message received and understood.' Zac's mouth had twitched.

Once on the first-floor landing, which was all creaking varnished floorboards and whitewashed walls, the

landlady led them past a number of doors to the end of
the passage where they saw a narrower door. She opened
this and they continued to follow her up an almost verti-
cally steep staircase, the middle of each tread worn to
a smooth depression by centuries of feet.

'Used to be the servants' quarters,' the landlady informed them over her shoulder. 'Poor things.' Then,
obviously realising her comment wasn't exactly con-
ducive to getting a good price for the room, she added,
''Course, in them days the attics were cold and draughty
places, windowless, most of them. We've had this done
up really nice, as you'll see.'

One thing was for sure, the landlady hadn't been
joking when she'd said the ceiling was low. Rachel had
to bend her head and when Zac reached the top stair
and stepped into the room, he was bent almost double.
That aside, the room was large—although a good third
was unusable, the ceiling height falling to no more than
two or three feet in places—and fully carpeted. What
looked like a custom-made double bed stood under two
roof lights, although these were shrouded with snow.
The legs of the bedstead were only six inches high so
that the bed virtually sat on the floor. One wall had open
shelving, along with a bar on which coat hangers hung—
presumably because a traditional wardrobe wouldn't
have fitted into the space—and a low coffee table by
the door held an electric kettle, cups and saucers and the
traditional hotel packets of coffee, tea and sugar, along
with several small packets of biscuits and tiny cartons
of UHT milk.

The room could have been termed quaint—if you
were a young child or extremely small adult. As it
was…

The landlady looked at their faces. 'There's nothing else.'

Rachel had been hoping for twin beds or at least a comfy armchair where she could curl up with a blanket. Groaning inwardly, she forced a polite smile. 'It's fine.'

'Well, I'll leave you to get sorted out and come down when you're ready, all right? There's a table for two by the fire free—you'll soon be nice and warm again.' The landlady smiled a beatific smile and bustled out.

Zac placed the suitcases on the floor, took off his overcoat and sat down on the bed so he could stretch his aching neck muscles. 'Never let it be said I don't know how to give a girl a good time,' he said wryly, glancing around their surroundings.

Rachel giggled. She felt slightly hysterical. She'd been right about the log fires, oak beams and so on—it was just the building in question was an old inn and she and Zac had been thrust into a situation she could never have foreseen. Kicking off her walking boots, she said, 'Shouldn't you phone and let them know we aren't going to make it tonight?'

He nodded, stretching his long legs and flexing his shoulders before digging his phone out of his pocket. Rachel wondered how perfectly natural actions could be so mouth-wateringly sexy where Zac was concerned. And how she was going to get through the next few hours without forgetting every good reason why she shouldn't sleep with him.

She pulled on her new boots and squatted down in front of the mirror on the wall to tidy her hair, reflecting it was the first time in her life she'd felt like a giant. Her knees were aching by the time she'd renewed her lipstick and straightened up. Zac was lying on the bed watching her, having finished his phone call. Ignoring the smouldering tawny eyes, she said, 'Shall we go and get something to eat? I'm starving.'

'Me too.'

She knew he wasn't referring to food but pretended she didn't. 'Was Martin OK about us not coming?' she asked for something to say, turning and reaching for her handbag.

'Of course. Half the guests haven't turned up apparently.' As she opened the bedroom door he uncoiled his long body and stood up—as best he could. 'I can't believe it's legal to ask money for a room like this,' he muttered, after bumping his head on the doorframe as he followed her down the perilous staircase. 'It's only fit for leprechauns.'

She turned to face him on the first-floor landing, slightly more at ease now they'd left their intimate little bird's nest. 'It's probably not legal. The landlady didn't strike me as someone who'd bother too much about things like that, or health and safety either.' She glanced at the landing window where the whirling snow was battering against the glass. 'Still, lucky for us it was available, all things considered.'

'Oh, don't get me wrong, I'm not complaining.' He reached out and smoothed a lock of hair from her cheek, his fingers stroking her throat for an infinitesimal moment. 'It's just not what I'd got in mind for you this weekend, that's all.'

Not what she'd had in mind either. Especially the double bed.

'I was going to wow you with Martin's mansion and his umpteen acres, including a trout lake and stables and what have you, not to mention the indoor leisure complex and swarm of servants. Instead...' his eyes narrowed sexily and his mouth curved in a self-derisive smile '...there's just me and Gulliver's room.'

Rachel's stomach flipped over. As a seduction technique it was very good. He'd obviously had a lot of practice in that department. So why, knowing that, did her traitorous body respond so fiercely? She cleared her throat, determined to gain control. And she might have done if Zac hadn't chosen that moment to kiss her again. Drawing her into his arms, he lifted her chin, tilting her face so he could gain full access to her mouth. The kiss wasn't threatening; in fact, it was gentle—an unbelievably slow, erotic exploration that melted her bones. The desire that had sent her blood racing from the first moment she'd set eyes on him became longing; he kissed better than Giles or any of her other boyfriends, better than she would have dreamt possible. All her fantasies rolled into one.

His lips caressed her throat, her eyelids, the corners of her mouth, sweeping away caution and reason so that when he took her lips again she kissed him back. His mouth was urgent, hungry, and the taste, the delicious smell of him spun in her head. He moved slightly, moulding her into him so she fitted more comfortably into his hard frame, and she felt his strength, his desire against her softness.

The sound of a door opening downstairs brought them apart. As someone came out into the hall below and then began to climb the stairs, Zac took her arm, moving her along the landing as though they'd just left their room. He seemed totally unperturbed and in control, and to Rachel's fevered senses it was like a sharp slap across the face.

She forced her mind into automatic so she could cope with returning the polite 'Good evening' the rosy-cheeked walker gave them as he passed at the top of the stairs, and then as she descended to the hall with Zac behind her, she clenched her teeth, breathing through her nose. This whole thing, their—what? flirtation, brief dalliance, game—meant little to Zac beyond a mild spot of intrigue to while away the spare hours while he was in England. His reaction to what she had considered the most mind-blowing experience of her life was proof of that. He hadn't felt an iota of what she had.

Tears pricked at the back of her eyes and she blinked them away fiercely, angry at her weakness. She was not going to cry; she was not going to give him any inkling of what that kiss had done to her. This had been a timely reminder from her guardian angel that men were as different from women as chalk to cheese. A man's emotions were all tied up with a certain part of his anatomy that—once satisfied—moved on to the next conquest. How many times did she have to learn the same lesson, for goodness' sake? She was stupid, so stupid.

Rachel marched through to the pub lounge without looking behind her or waiting for Zac, pushing open the door and stepping into the noisy room with her head held high. Jennie and Susan would have recognised the attitude of bravado: they'd witnessed it many times in the aftermath of Giles's betrayal. They would have understood that from childhood Rachel had become adept at disguising her feelings and that wearing her heart on her sleeve was alien to her. She walked over to the table by the fire the landlady had mentioned and sat down, Zac a step behind her. Looking up at him, she gave a brilliant smile. 'This is nice.' She held out her hands to the crackling flames.

His mouth quirked attractively. 'You're easily pleased.'

How right he was, but she wouldn't make the same mistake again. Looking around him, she said, 'The landlady's waving two menus at us, I think she wants you to collect them. And I'll have a glass of red wine while you're there.'

There was a shadow of puzzlement in the golden eyes—he had clearly picked up that something had changed. He stared at her for a long moment, his smile dying, and then turned and went to the bar. She continued to look at him, her peripheral vision taking in the little stir he'd caused among the female component of the walkers.

Her mouth tightened. They were stuck here for tonight, that was as clear as the nose on her face, but come morning she would make it plain she had no intention of continuing to the house party. She wanted to go home. And he might be able to charm the birds out of the trees but tonight he was going to find himself with one girl who was well and truly immune to the great Zac Lawson. And he could put that little experience in his pipe and smoke it.

CHAPTER SIX

ZAC CAME BACK WITH A bottle of wine and two glasses, the menus tucked under one arm. After handing her a menu and pouring them both a glass of wine, he settled back in his chair and said expressionlessly, 'OK, what have I done?'

She waited for two or three seconds before raising her eyes from the menu. 'I'm sorry? I don't know what you mean.'

'You're a different person suddenly.'

She raised her eyebrows. 'I have no idea what you're talking about. I think we need to order, don't we? It's late.'

'Is it because I've messed up the weekend and we're stuck here?' he asked levelly. 'Are you mad at me?'

Her chin tilted a fraction higher. 'Of course not. And you haven't messed up the weekend. Even you can't control the weather. Now, we really do need to decide on food.'

He surveyed her silently for enough time for Rachel to squirm inwardly, but she was determined not to show any weakness. 'Then it must be because I kissed you,' he said thoughtfully. 'We were OK before then. Did you assume I was preparing the ground for the full deployment when we go back to the room?'

Rather than him guess the truth, that would do. She took a sip of wine before she dared look him in the eyes. 'Weren't you?' she challenged.

There was another long pause. 'I don't know,' he said with a frown. 'I kissed you because I wanted to, because I long to kiss or touch you every moment I'm with you, and if you want the truth I would very much like to sleep with you. I can't help that, Rachel. I'm a man. However...' There was a distinct pause. 'I'm not an animal. I've never once taken a woman to bed who wasn't one hundred per cent willing, so you have nothing to fear from me.'

She didn't doubt he'd never had to cajole or manipulate a woman; there was probably a queue round the block of willing females ready to warm his bed. Coolly, she said, 'I'll have the steak and kidney pie with onion mash and seasonal vegetables,' as she handed the menu back to him. 'You order at the bar.'

'I'm aware of that,' he said, equally coolly.

She was behaving very badly. As she watched Zac talking to the landlady she suddenly felt very small and very alone in the crowded room. She'd bet she'd get no argument from him tomorrow about taking her home, he probably couldn't wait to get rid of her. Her mouth drooped at the corners and her gaze turned inwards. Somehow her life hadn't turned out at all as she'd expected when she and Jennie and Susan had been carefree students. She didn't profess to be anything special, far from it, but she'd thought by the age of twenty-seven she would be married, probably with the prospect of a family high on the agenda. She'd never envisaged a lifetime career in marketing.

Had she been too choosy with the men she'd dated before Giles? She pictured one or two in her mind. But if the spark wasn't there, it wasn't there, surely? She'd liked them, had had fun and some good times, but she'd never been tempted to think of them as 'the one'.

She hadn't been aware Zac had left the bar but when he slid into his seat, saying, 'It's OK, Rachel. Really,' her head shot up to meet his gaze. His face was impassive.

She made a gesture of confusion. 'I'm sorry?'

'I'm not going to ravish you in the middle of the night when you're asleep or leap on you the minute we get back to the room. I promise. Now, could you please stop looking as though every moment with me is torture, because you're making the landlady think we don't appreciate the luxury of our surroundings.'

She looked into his eyes, saw the hidden laughter in the golden orbs and wanted to kick him. 'She does not.'

'Oh, yes, she does,' he informed her solemnly. '"Zac", she said—we're on first-name terms now—"it must be my inn that's putting that expression on your girlfriend's face because it couldn't be you. You're too charming, too wonderful, too altogether fascinating for it to be you."'

'Don't be so ridiculous.' She glared at him. 'And I am *not* your girlfriend.'

'Ah, but she doesn't know that. Your eagerness to share a room with me didn't help either. In her eyes we're definitely an item,' he said with an air of satisfaction.

Rachel had made the mistake of taking a sip of wine. Now she spluttered and choked a little before banging the glass down on the table. 'I most definitely was *not* eager to share a room with you. It just so happens that it's the only room left in the place and I was tired and cold and hungry.'

'*I* know that.' His tone was soothing, exaggeratedly so. 'But the landlady doesn't. She said—'

'I really don't care what the landlady was supposed to have said, and I don't believe she said anything anyway.'

He smiled, a genuine smile, one that crinkled his eyes and accelerated Rachel's breathing. '"Oh, ye of little faith…"'

Trying to maintain a glare, she took another sip of wine. She needed the boost to her system. 'I'll sleep in a chair down here tonight,' she said waspishly. 'That'll settle things.'

'No can do. Fire and safety regulations.'

'You're making that up,' she accused, not fooled by his innocent expression. 'Like the rest of this silly conversation.'

'Would I?' he drawled lazily, not in the least put out.

Impossible man. Impossible situation. 'Absolutely.'

One of the walkers, a healthy, tanned, attractive blonde girl in tight jeans and an even tighter T-shirt, sashayed slowly past their table, staring at Zac with what Rachel considered brazen interest. Suddenly she felt as deflated as a pricked balloon. The girl was brimming over with eager exuberance and self-confidence, and she was lovely. She wouldn't have any hang-ups about sleeping with a handsome single man; in fact, she'd probably make the first move in the bed department.

Rachel watched the high ponytail of sleek curls bob as the girl passed, her perfect little derrière displayed to maximum advantage in the snug denim. She didn't look a day over eighteen and she oozed life and vivacity, a boldness and assurance about her that suggested she was happily comfortable inside her skin. That was the kind of woman Zac should be with.

'What are you thinking?'

'What?' Startled, her eyes snapped to his.

'The look on your face...' His voice hesitated and stopped. His golden eyes held hers. After what seemed an age, he said softly, 'You're an enigma, do you know that? I find myself feeling like a schoolboy when I'm with you, wanting to do something outrageous to impress you.'

She stared at him, too taken aback to hide it.

'And I don't know why,' he continued, still in the same quiet tone. 'You're beautiful, but I've known many beautiful women in my time and none of them have affected me the way you do. I want to know everything you think and feel, what makes you happy and what makes you sad, what you like and don't like, what's made you into the woman you are.'

Mesmerised, she murmured, 'I'm not beautiful.'

'Oh, but you are, in a gentle, soft and very dangerous way. A way that makes a man forget who he is and what he wants out of life,' he added wryly, a self-derisive quirk to his lips.

He couldn't be talking about her. Rachel's eyes fell to her hands. Siren material she definitely was not.

'So, you see, I need to understand you but every time I think I've found out one facet it changes, like the clouds on a windy day. Which is...unsettling.' He gave a growl of a laugh. 'Very unsettling.'

Unthinkingly, Rachel finished her glass of wine and watched his strong, capable fingers as he poured her another. 'You're making me out to be someone I'm not,' she whispered when he settled back in his chair, his face broodingly intent on hers. 'I'm very ordinary, as it happens.'

Again the growl of a laugh rumbled. 'Rachel, you're many things, and a whole host of them damn exasperating, but ordinary you are most definitely not.'

Her chin rose. 'If I'm such a trial, why have you persisted in asking me out? Wouldn't it have been easier to walk away?'

'I told you, I need to suss you out if I'm going to have any peace of mind when I go back home.' His voice had lost all amusement. 'And you know I will go back, don't you?' He leaned forward. 'I have to. My work, family, friends—my *life's* in Canada.'

They stared at each other wordlessly, the silence stretching until Rachel was ready to scream. From somewhere she found the strength to speak at last. 'I haven't asked you to stay, Zac.'

His mouth tightened for a moment, then relaxed. 'True.'

Self-preservation urged her on. 'Nor would I,' she added, sounding brutal even to her own ears. 'The last thing I want is—'

'Me?' he cut in drily.

'A relationship. With *anyone*,' she emphasised softly. 'The thing with Giles…' She paused for a moment. 'Well, it made me realise I don't want to put myself in the same position again. Not for a long, long time anyway.'

He refilled his own glass and before the conversation could continue, one of the girls from behind the bar came bustling up with two steaming plates. 'Two steak and kidney pies?' she enquired cheerily, as though the place was full of customers who'd recently ordered. Depositing a plate in front of each of them, she added,

'The veg and mash are on their way, all right? Is there anything else I can get you?'

Zac raised his eyebrows at Rachel and when she shook her head, he smiled at the waitress. 'Nothing, thanks. This looks great. Smells good too.'

The girl smiled back, lowering her voice and bending towards them as she said, 'The food's fabulous here, that's what makes it so popular. Ken, the chef, owns the place too and he used to be head chef at one of the big London hotels till him and Maggie...' she gestured towards the landlady with a jerk of her head '...got married. They've built up a real good reputation,' she added proudly. 'Folk come from miles around to eat here.'

Rachel smiled. There was something ingenuous about the young girl's enthusiasm. 'You obviously like working here.'

'Love it,' she answered promptly. 'Life's too short to stay anywhere you don't like, isn't it? Live for today, that's what I say. Make the most of each minute and there's no regrets.'

She gave them a beaming smile and then, as another girl brought the dishes of mashed potato and vegetables, took them from her, placed them in the centre of the table and walked back to the bar. Rachel gazed after her; she was young to be a sage.

'She's right, you know.' Zac had just taken a bite of his pie while Rachel helped herself to the mash and veg. 'Dead right.'

'About the food?' she asked, passing him a serving spoon.

'No. Well, that too, but I meant the living-for-today bit.' He eyed her innocently. 'Perhaps that's what we should do this weekend? Live for the moment with no thought to tomorrow?'

She managed a creditable laugh. 'Why is it men always come up with that one when they've got an ulterior motive in mind?' she said lightly, glad he had taken her earlier rebuff without sulking. Giles had sulked. Often.

He'd heaped up his plate and now he grinned at her. He looked big and dark and so handsome he took her breath away. She wondered what he'd say if she told him that from the first moment they'd met she'd had wildly erotic and definitely X-rated fantasies about him. Not that she ever would.

She swallowed hard, fighting to remain unmoved by the sexual magnetism he exerted as naturally as breathing. And failing miserably. She had a mental picture of the big double bed in their room and swallowed again, panic slicing in, hot and strong.

'This is delicious—try some. The pie's packed with meat.'

Zac was totally relaxed and eating his meal with relish, clearly untroubled by the kind of thoughts assailing her. And in spite of all he'd said, he seemed pretty unperturbed by her ultimate rejection of him too. Men really were a different species, she thought with a mixture of anger and bewilderment. And then she caught a heavenly whiff of the steak and kidney pie that made her mouth water, at the same time as her stomach reminded her she hadn't eaten for aeons.

To hell with it. She picked up her knife and fork and tucked in. If you can't beat 'em, join 'em.

The steak and kidney pie was swiftly followed by apple crumble and custard, and by the coffee stage of the meal Rachel was sitting toasting her toes in front of the fire, listening to the merry group of walkers hollering out one Christmas carol after another. They were a lively bunch but tuneless.

The landlady had brought two brandies with the coffee, insisting they were the promised 'warm-up' drinks and on the house, and with her stomach full and the wine having taken the edge off her worry about the night ahead, Rachel felt almost mellow as she sipped the spirit.

'Against all the odds, this is nice.' Zac had taken off his jacket and loosened his tie, undoing the first couple of buttons of his shirt. It had caused her a few momentary problems at the time but her body had just about adjusted. She glanced at him as he spoke and the golden gaze was waiting for her.

Rachel smiled. 'Yes, it is.' They'd talked of amusing, inconsequential things during the meal, putting the previous tenseness behind them by unspoken mutual consent. If they could just stay here like this all night she'd be OK, she thought now with wry humour. But that double bed loomed large.

Zac swallowed the last of his brandy. 'Fancy another?' he offered, rising to his feet. 'We haven't got far to go to bed.'

Two glasses of wine and a brandy was really her limit, she'd never been able to drink alcohol at the same level as most of the other students at uni and her tolerance had got less since. Tonight, though, satisfyingly warm and replete, a spirit of recklessness took hold. 'Lovely.' She held out her glass.

'That was said with the air of someone who's stoking up some Dutch courage to face the trial ahead. Am I right?'

She frowned at him. 'Don't be silly, Zac.'

'But you make me want to be silly, Rachel. To say

silly things, to act silly, anything to shake that cool reserve of yours,' he said mildly.

She stared at him open-mouthed, a part of her thrilled he imagined she could feel remotely cool around him. If he only knew... But she was so thankful he didn't.

His lips twitched at her expression but he said nothing more, turning and walking to the bar with their empty brandy glasses. Rachel noticed the blonde walker immediately leave her group and make her way to his side, presumably on the pretext of ordering more drinks. She wanted to look away but something compelled her to watch. The girl said something to Zac to get his attention and, as he looked at her, did the full femme fatale thing, complete with fluttering eyelashes and pouty lips.

'So what am I? Invisible?' Rachel muttered to herself.

Zac's reply was short and the next moment he'd taken their replenished glasses and was walking back to her. Rachel had a brief glimpse of a lovely but definitely disgruntled face before he handed her her drink, his body blocking her view.

It was the alcohol that must have loosened her tongue because normally she wouldn't have dreamt of saying anything, but once he had sat down she found herself asking, 'What did that girl at the bar say to you?'

'Girl?' he replied absently. 'Oh, the girl. She wondered if we'd like to join them, that's all.'

'And you said no.'

'Of course.' His brows drew together. 'Why? You don't want to party with that lot, do you?'

About as much as swimming with sharks. 'Not particularly, no,' she answered carefully.

'Good.' The slight frown cleared. 'The landlady's just told me she's put a couple of hot-water bottles in our bed to warm it through, although she's quite sure it's aired.'

The words, 'our bed' were all that registered.

'Nice of her, wasn't it?' Zac murmured, leaning back in his chair and stretching his long legs out in front of him.

Allowing her hair to fall about her cheeks to hide the colour she knew was staining her face, Rachel twisted sideways and held out her hands to the glowing fire. 'Very nice,' she agreed expressionlessly. 'She's done her best to make us welcome.'

'She asked if we wanted a cooked breakfast and I said yes. It's served between eight and ten apparently but if we're a bit late she said not to worry, they're pretty flexible.'

Our bed. Hot-water bottles. Breakfast. The words ricocheted about her head. Altogether too cosy, too seductive. She forced herself to take a sip of the brandy and turn back to face him after the hot colour that flooded her cheeks subsided. He was lying back in his chair, eyes closed, one hand holding his glass and the other hanging loosely. The epitome of casual comfortableness. A man at ease with his surroundings and himself.

It was the first time she had been able to study him without the tawny eyes watching her. His dark hair gleamed blue-black in the subdued lighting, and his lashes were thick and long where they rested on the high chiselled cheekbones. Wasted on a man, she thought irrelevantly. The glow from the fire had picked out a tiny scar on his chin. It was paler than the rest of his tanned skin and Rachel wondered why she hadn't noticed it before and how he'd got it. Playing some kind of sport probably, she decided. He was clearly a man who liked to keep fit. Did he work out? She let her eyes run over the broad muscled shoulders and down to the flat waistband of his trousers. Oh, yes. Not an ounce of fat on this body. He definitely was familiar with a gym.

When the tawny eyes opened to stare straight into hers, she blinked, but this time refused to blush. With what she considered admirable coolness in the circumstances, she said lightly, 'It isn't very polite to fall asleep on your dinner companion.'

He shifted in the chair, sitting straighter, and every nerve in her body responded. 'I wasn't asleep,' he protested lazily. 'Merely shutting my eyes for a moment.'

'That's what old men say when they take a snooze.'

'I'm not an old man, Rachel.' His voice was smoky, husky. 'I'll prove it if you like. Upstairs.'

She'd asked for that. From some unexpected but welcome reserve of strength she managed a tinkle of a laugh. 'And if I don't like? What then?'

'Then I won't,' he said, perfectly seriously.

The faint, sexy Canadian burr that laced the deep voice caused a funny little shiver deep inside. She had to clear her throat before she came back with, 'Regretfully, I'll have to pass on your kind offer,' but even to her own ears she didn't quite carry off the light tone.

'Believe me, the regret's all mine.'

No, it wasn't. She finished her brandy, needing the warmth it provided. It so wasn't.

CHAPTER SEVEN

'So, how do we do this?'

'What?' They'd just come back to the room and Rachel knew nothing in her life thus far had prepared her for being in a bedroom with Zac Lawson on a dark winter's night. A cat on a hot tin roof was nothing compared to how jumpy she felt.

'The mechanics of getting ready for bed,' Zac said patiently. 'I don't know about you but I'd like a shower so that's a trip to the bathroom on the floor below. Do you want to go first?'

She didn't know what she wanted. Well, she did, but it wasn't helpful. Forcing her skittish mind into action, she thought swiftly. If she went first she could wash and brush her teeth, and then change into her pyjamas when Zac was having his shower. 'Yes, please.' She grabbed her toiletry bag and one of the towels the landlady had placed at the foot of the bed. 'I'll be as quick as I can.'

'Take as long as you like. There's no hurry.'

Zac had thrown himself on the bed and was lying with his hands beneath his head, surveying her with amused eyes. For once she was too flustered to be annoyed.

The bathroom turned out to be a huge, old-fashioned affair but charming in its own way. The cast-iron bath was an enormous thing on quaint little legs and Rachel gazed at it longingly. A long hot soak was just what she needed right now to relax tense, taut muscles. However, with Zac waiting for his turn, she contented herself with a quick shower and was in and out within two minutes. After brushing her teeth and taking off her make-up, she surveyed her naked face in the mirror.

She looked clean and slightly pink. Wholesome. And she didn't want to look wholesome. She wanted to exude sexiness like Jennie or possess the delicate, ethereal beauty of Susan. She shut her eyes tightly for a moment. But she didn't. And growing up with two blonde bombshells of sisters, you'd have thought she'd be done crying for the moon. She was what she was and normally she was content with that. Her eyes opened. Tonight was different. She longed to be someone else tonight.

Zac was lying watching the news on the small TV the room boasted when she opened the door. 'It's pretty bad,' he said, nodding at the picture of deep snow and abandoned cars on the screen. 'And according to the forecast there's no signs of it letting up yet. Looks like we could be stuck here for a couple of days. Still…' he smiled wickedly '…the bed's comfortable.'

No. Please, no. She might just about be able to get through one night without forgetting every principle she'd lived by for the last years, but two or three?

He had rolled off the bed onto his feet as he spoke; now he walked to where she was standing, still just inside the door. 'Nice,' he murmured softly, touching her flushed cheek with one finger and then tracing the outline of her mouth. 'Like a scrubbed little girl all squeaky clean and ready for bed.'

Great. She'd been spot on in the bathroom, then.

He stroked the shining fall of her hair, his voice pre-occupied when he breathed, 'Is the water hot?'

'The…the water? Oh, the water. Yes, it's fine.' Don't stammer and stutter, she told herself in disgust. What's the matter with you? Act your age, even if you don't look it.

The matter was Zac. Her eyes had fastened of their own volition on the tiny scar on his chin and her senses registered the way the black stubble coming through avoided the spot. And he always smelt so good, she told herself helplessly as the strength seeped from her knees. Why did he always have to smell so good? All the odds were on his side.

She knew he was going to kiss her but when he did she still wasn't ready for it. His lips were firm and confident against hers, moving with a leisurely expertise that made her tremble deep inside. His arms were round her and gently and repetitively his fingers began stroking her back, moving in light circles over her tense shoulders and down the concavity of her spine. It felt good, much too good, and as he deepened the kiss she kissed him back. Against her softness she felt the involuntary hardening of Zac's body and experienced a moment's primal pleasure that wanted her. She wound herself closer instinctively.

When he finally broke the contact between them he was breathing heavily, his gaze narrowed and glittering as he stared down into her face. 'You taste so good.'

Rachel swayed, then stepped back a pace out of his body warmth so she could think again. 'Zac, I don't—'

'Sleep with a man you've only known for a day or two,' he finished for her. 'I know that, Rachel. I know the kind of woman you are.' He raked his hair back from his forehead and took a visibly deep breath. 'I'd better make that shower a cold one,' he said with a wryness that would have made her smile if she'd hadn't been feeling so wretched.

As it was, she stood quite still while he collected his towel and bag, and even after he'd left the room she remained where she was for a full minute before sitting down on the bed with a plump. She still wasn't quite sure how she'd got herself into such a mess, she thought weakly. And a mess it was. From her teenage years she had always known she would have to be in love before she could allow total intimacy, and here she was serious considering sleeping with Zac in every sense of the word. It was a relief to admit it at last. And this a man who had told her quite clearly he would be gone shortly, back to Canada and his life and work there.

She made a sound in her throat, a cross between a moan and a groan, and then, aware the minutes were ticking by, jumped up and rummaged through her suitcase for her night things.

And it wasn't as if she didn't know what Zac—and the majority of the whole male species, come to it—was like. He wouldn't need to be remotely fond of her to indulge in anything and everything—that was the difference between the sexes. Of course, not all men went in for one-night stands or casual sex, but with most men if it was there on offer, they'd take it.

Rachel stripped off her clothes with trembling fingers and pulled on her silk pyjamas, wishing she'd brought a pair with more covering power than the camisole top and shorts gave. Scrambling into bed, she pulled the covers up to her chin and found she was trembling uncontrollably. This was ridiculous; it was, it was *absolutely* ridiculous. In spite of herself, a nervous giggle escaped. In all her wildest dreams of spending the night with a man, this scenario had never occurred.

She strained her ears but could hear nothing outside the room. Tucked away as it was at the top of the inn and with thick solid walls to muffle any sound, it was its own little world. Her cold feet found one of the hot-water bottles and as the warmth slowly permeated her flesh, she found herself relaxing into the soft bed. Zac was right, it *was* comfortable.

What would Jennie and Susan say if they could see her now, stretched out in a big double bed and waiting for Zac? Again a hysterical squeak of laughter emerged, and she warned herself to get a grip. Laughing like a hyena was not attractive.

The news programme was now showing the rescue earlier that day of a horse and rider who'd ended up in a ditch. Apparently when they'd come to a gate, which the rider had leant forward to open, the horse had automatically taken a step backwards to allow the gate to swing open, but what it had thought to be solid ground, due to the snow had, in fact, been a deep ditch. Fortunately the rider had managed to spring to the side and clamber out without the horse—who'd ended up with all four legs sticking up in the air—kicking her. And after the horse had been tranquillised by a local vet, they'd managed to haul it out with a small crane, merely muddy and with a few cuts and bruises. But, the newscaster emphasised, the danger of the snow wasn't to be underestimated. Keep warm, stay at home and don't venture out.

Now they tell me. Rachel flexed her toes. This bout of snow had turned out to be positively lethal as far as she was concerned.

She was wide awake but cosily comfortable when Zac opened the bedroom door. Immediately her heart began to hammer in her ribcage and every muscle tightened. Not that he was undressed or looked any different from when he'd left the room, except his hair was damp and he hadn't bothered to button his shirt. Actually, that made him very different. And infinitely more sexy, she thought desperately.

'Look what Santa Claus has brought me this year,' he drawled softly, the mocking tilt to his lips telling her he was fully aware of her wide eyes. 'A very special bed-warmer.'

'It's not Christmas yet,' she pointed out as he walked over to the bed, 'and believe me, Zac, I'm not your bed-warmer.'

'But you're in my bed and you're warm. That's a good start.'

Rachel wanted to come back with some pithy retort but he chose that moment to take his shirt off and her mouth went as dry as a bone. She couldn't take her eyes off his thickly muscled torso, the tight black curls on his chest narrowing to a thin line that disappeared into the waistband of his trousers. He was gorgeous, she thought helplessly. *Gorgeous*.

He sat down on the bed and pulled off his socks, throwing them onto the top of his suitcase, which was lying flat on the floor. Standing up once more, he un-buckled his belt and unzipped his trousers, and at that point Rachel came to her senses enough to look away. She'd been ogling him, she thought in horror, and then, as the trousers followed the socks, couldn't resist a swift look under her eyelashes. He was wearing nothing but black boxer shorts and they were of the clinging kind. And he looked beyond good. Hard, powerful thighs, lithe, tanned legs and—as she'd expected—not an ounce of surplus fat anywhere.

Her breathing was shallow and for the life of her she couldn't swallow past the constriction in her throat. Staring at her hands clasped on top of the cover, she was incredibly grateful she was lying down because her oxygen supply was all but gone.

'Slight problem in that I don't wear pyjamas.'

She made the mistake of looking at him. He was grinning at her but the boxer shorts were still in place. She didn't know whether to be relieved or disappointed.

'I presume you'd rather I kept these on?'

She nodded because she knew if she tried to talk it would emerge as gobbledegook, and wouldn't he just love that?

'Sure?' He stood there, practically naked, smiling at her.

Oh, but he had a body to die for. Which was why he was flaunting it with such magnificent unconcern presumably. 'Yes,' she squeaked. 'I'm sure.' Liar, a voice in her head accused.

'OK.' He padded across and turned off the light and the next moment he'd slid into bed beside her.

Rachel stiffened, as rigid as a board. She couldn't help it. The light in the bedroom now came courtesy of the TV, and when Zac reached for the remote and switched it off, the room was bathed in darkness. She didn't dare move, she didn't dare even *breathe* as he settled himself more comfortably, his body touching hers for a heart-stopping moment.

'Silk?' he said after a few painful seconds had ticked by.

She cleared her throat and took a lungful of much-needed air. 'Sorry?' It emerged as a strangled croak.

'Your nightwear. It felt like silk.'

She could tell his head had turned on the pillow to

look at her, even though she couldn't see him. Drawing on all her resources, she managed to say, fairly coherently, 'It is.'

'What colour?' he murmured, very softly.

'Sorry?' she said again, although she'd heard him perfectly.

'What colour is the silk? If I'm not allowed to see, the least you can do is describe what you're wearing. Or would you rather I turn on the light and take a peek?'

'Blue.' She held onto the bedclothes like grim death.

'Deep blue or light blue?'

'Deep blue.' A deep, violet blue actually, with black lace round the top of the camisole and bordering the splits in the side of the shorts, which came almost to waist level. Enough to protect her modesty should the worse happen, but only just. She wondered if he could hear her heart banging.

His grunt expressed satisfaction. 'Like your eyes.'

Another few moments went by before he murmured, 'I forgot to ask, do you snore?'

She could hear the amusement in his voice and tried to match his tone, although with her nerves as taut as piano wire it wasn't easy. 'How would I know? I'd be asleep if I did, wouldn't I?'

'And your previous boyfriends have never complained?'

It threw her and she hesitated just a fraction too long before she said, 'No, no they haven't,' even as she asked herself why she hadn't come right out and admitted she hadn't slept with a man before. It had been the perfect opportunity.

The answer was there immediately. She didn't want him to think any less of her. In his world of sophisticated and cosmopolitan women, a twenty-seven-year-old virgin would be an oddity at best and a freak at worst. She wasn't ashamed of what she was, it was her choice after all, but nevertheless…

Aware his stillness had a different quality to it, and with the air so charged it almost crackled, she hoped against hope he'd let the conversation drop. The silence lengthened, quivering like a living entity. After what seemed an eternity to Rachel's fraught nerves, it was almost a relief when he said softly, 'Rachel, have you slept with a man before?'

She was so glad it was dark. Wrinkling up her face in an agony of embarrassment, she waited until she knew her voice wouldn't tremble. 'No.' She opened her eyes wide.

He swore softly, which didn't exactly help the way she was feeling, but immediately said, 'Sorry. Really, sorry, but I just didn't see that one coming.' A brief pause ensued before he spoke again. 'Is it because you're frightened of sex?'

She hadn't thought it could get any worse but she supposed logically it was the next obvious question. He was clearly wondering if she'd been abused or something. Rachel swallowed. 'No, nothing like that, I've just been waiting—' she knew this was going to sound absurd to a man like Zac '—for the right one, I suppose. The one I want to spend the rest of my life with.'

There was an even longer pause. Then his voice came softly and with a thread of something she couldn't put a name to. 'That's one hell of an effective chastity belt.'

Which translated as saying he wouldn't touch her with a bargepole now. She squeezed her eyes to stop the tears from falling. What was she crying for anyway? This was absolutely the best thing, wasn't it? He was going to disappear out of her life in a couple of weeks and if she'd given herself to him, how would she feel when he left?

She thought she'd done pretty well in disguising the tears, it was pitch black in the room after all, but after a minute or so, when she'd surreptitiously wiped her eyes with the back of her hand a couple of times, he suddenly said, 'You aren't crying, are you? Hell, Rachel, tell me you aren't crying.'

She couldn't answer, not without breaking down completely and howling like a banshee, which would be the final humiliation.

She heard him groan and mutter something under his breath that sounded very much like a string of oaths, and the next moment she found herself gathered against a hard male body as he cradled her against him and began stroking her hair in a soothing, rhythmic caress. 'It's OK, sweet Rachel, it's OK.' His voice was soft and tender, the mockery she'd feared absent. 'Don't cry, honey. I'm not going to hurt you.'

She wanted to tell him that it wasn't that, that she was crying more for what she was missing along with a hundred and one other things she couldn't put a name to, but held close to him like this she couldn't say a word. Her cheek was resting on his broad chest and her fingers had curled involuntarily into his body hair; she could hear the steady thud of his heart and his skin smelt of shower gel. Heaven on earth...

'Your hair still carries the scent of apples,' he said above her head, huskiness in his voice. 'Apple blossom on a spring day, fresh and beautiful and sun-kissed. *You're* beautiful, Rachel, but you don't quite believe that, do you?'

She didn't know what she believed at this moment,

only what she felt, and that was the stirrings of a desire so powerful it took her breath away. His muscled body was hard and strong, its male angles and planes alien but so right. She wanted to stretch out on him, melt into him, feel him envelop and touch and enclose her. She wanted to feel him inside her, loving her.

'This guy you were involved with, the one who let you down so badly, don't let him spoil your life.' She felt him nuzzle the top of her head and instinctively lifted her face. For a split second she felt him stiffen and then his lips claimed hers, firm and warm and seductively sure. His mouth played with hers, teasing her into a response that amazed her, or would have done if she had been thinking clearly. As it was, the more intimate the kiss grew, the more she abandoned all reserve.

The darkness, the soft warm bed, his hard masculine body and what his lips and hands were doing to her swept her off into another world of touch and taste, a place of sensual excitement where everyday life didn't exist. She kissed him back because it seemed good and natural and what she'd been waiting for all her life without knowing it.

When her head fell back a little, Zac rained soft burning kisses on her chin and the exposed line of her throat, his hands cupping her breasts through the thin silk and stroking her engorged nipples. She gasped, and Zac took advantage of her open lips to return to her mouth, his tongue running riot with her heightened senses.

He caressed her with exquisitely controlled sensuality and a pleasure totally unfeigned, the soft pads of his fingertips injecting needles of sensation until she was aflame and the kiss had deepened to a kind of consummation. He pulled her more completely into him until she could feel every inch of his arousal, but then almost immediately pushed her away, flinging back the covers and moving to sit on the side of the bed.

'Zac?' she whispered tremblingly, still in the throes of desire. 'What's wrong? Have I done something wrong?'

'Give me a minute.' His voice was hoarse.

She lay still, unable to believe for a moment or two he had stopped, the ache in her body so strong it took all her will not to reach out for him. Slowly the desire was replaced by hot humiliation. How could she have encouraged him—and that's what she'd done, she thought in an agony of shame—to make love to her when she knew this could be nothing more than a passing fancy for Zac? He hadn't pretended he loved her or even that he was going to be around for a while; he'd been brutally honest from the start in making it clear this was a one-off trip and nothing more. And she had…

She shut her eyes tightly at what she'd done. If he hadn't stopped, they would have been fully intimate— she knew that as well as he did. But he had stopped. She wanted to squirm with embarrassment and pain. He hadn't wanted her as much as she had wanted him; he had been able to control his mind and body and prove he could take her or leave her—literally.

After what seemed an eternity she felt him move but he didn't lie down again, sitting up in bed as he drew the covers over his legs. 'I'm sorry about that,' he said quietly. 'It seems where you're concerned, my control isn't what it should be.'

'It—it was my fault.'

'Hardly,' he said wryly. 'I knew the score, you'd just made it plain how things are with you, and I let…' he drew in a long shuddering breath '…the situation escalate out of control.'

Rachel drew in a long breath herself. She felt a bit better that he'd obviously had a struggle to stop.

'I didn't intend—' He stopped abruptly and from the way he moved she was sure he had raked his hand through his hair. 'No, that's not true. When we turned off the light I *did* intend to sweep away your defences. I was arrogant enough to presume this guy who'd let you down had soured your view of the male sex and I guess I thought I was the man to bring you back into dating mode again.' He gave a bark of a laugh. 'I thought we'd have a good time together, that I'd heal a few hurts. But when you told me you were a virgin—and why—that changed things.'

Now she did squirm.

'I don't want to be the one who takes that away from you, Rachel. Not when I can't offer you anything real in return.'

Well, that was telling her anyway, she thought with a sudden flash of anger. No dressing it up. The anger provided welcome adrenalin. 'You've always been very honest,' she said stiffly. 'And I've known all along you're only in England for a short time. You made that clear from our first meeting.'

'The thing is, Rachel…' He hesitated, then went on, 'I'm not looking for what you are. I've done the commitment thing once and once was enough. More than enough. I don't want to be in that kind of situation again.'

Oh, yeah, she thought waspishly. The old 'I need to be free to play the field' argument. A completely up-front attitude so any woman foolish enough to fall for him had no come-back when he said goodbye. No tears, no regrets, no recriminations. A different approach from the one Giles had but still at heart the same selfish me-

me-me perspective. How did she manage to find these sorts of men? she asked herself as hurt sliced through her. Or did they find her? Did she have some sort of aura that attracted the shallow, don't-give-a-damn types? 'I understand,' she said tightly. 'And you don't have to explain to me.'

'You don't and I do,' he shot back so swiftly it made her jump. 'I was married once and it didn't work out. We...' He stopped again, taking an audible breath. 'No, I need to start from the beginning. I met Moira when I was eighteen and she was seventeen. Two kids, that's all we were. Ten months later we were married because a baby was on the way. By that time we knew the thing between us had burnt itself out but neither of us wanted her to have an abortion, neither did we want the child growing up without both its parents. Rightly or wrongly, we'd agreed we'd provide a stable home for our child but be free to see other people as long as we were discreet. Crazy, looking back, but like I said we were young and crass.'

He'd been *married*? Rachel was unprepared for the way the news affected her, like a hard punch in the solar plexus.

'Even in the months leading up to the birth, I knew it wasn't going to work. She was my wife and that had changed things somehow. The thought of her seeing someone else or me having an affair had become... unacceptable. Moira pretended to agree; she was pregnant and clearly not looking around anyway. Then Josh was born after a long labour that suddenly went terribly wrong.'

There was a moment's screaming silence. Rachel found she was holding her breath.

'There were complications,' he said expressionlessly.

'He had the cord round his neck four times and no one had known. He never took breath. He was perfect, beautiful, but he never had a chance.'

This time when he stopped Rachel stared into the darkness in horror. She felt gut-wrenchingly sorry for Zac and disgusted with herself and the assumptions she'd made. 'I'm so sorry,' she said chokily, putting out a tentative hand. She found his arm, felt his muscles bunch beneath her fingers. 'That's terrible.'

'It was a long time ago.'

His voice was flat, wooden, which said only too clearly that it could have been yesterday as far as he was concerned. Rachel couldn't think of anything to say that wasn't horribly inadequate to the situation.

'On top of Josh's death, the birth had revealed Moira had a heart condition—a bad one. A few weeks after the funeral she had a heart transplant, but it didn't work as well as some and she was…not exactly an invalid, but not completely healthy either. But she had a good life, meeting her friends for lunch and shopping and generally indulging herself. Of course, in view of her illness, there was no way I could broach the matter of a divorce and she didn't seem to want one. Life went on. After two years I was beginning to feel I was going mad—trapped in a loveless marriage, playing the nurse rather than the husband when I was home from work, putting up with her rages when she blamed me for getting her pregnant, which had made her ill. She rarely mentioned Josh, it was as though he had never existed, but I put that down to the way she was dealing with her grief. Everyone copes in different ways.'

'You don't have to say any more if it's too painful.' Rachel squeezed his arm. 'Really, Zac, there's no need.'

As though she hadn't spoken, he continued, 'Two years to the day she had the transplant, she had a massive heart attack while lunching with a friend of hers. She died within minutes. At the funeral I met the friend. His name was Jack. Their affair had been going on for some months and apparently there had been someone else before him. She'd told him I was violent and used to knock her about—apparently I'd said I'd kill her if she ever left. He didn't even know she'd ever had a son, and I still don't know if she ever loved or grieved for our baby. Maybe she blamed him too for making her ill. But he was just a little boy.'

'Zac, I—I don't know what to say.' At some point he had moved his arm from her fingers and now she didn't know what to do, whether to reach out to him again or remain still.

'You don't need to say anything. I merely wanted to make you understand that commitment and marriage and a family is a route I'll never go down, that's all. I can't...' He paused and she knew the iron control had slipped for a second. 'I can't go there,' he continued huskily. 'That's why it would have been wrong of me to destroy the dream you have of giving yourself to the man you intend to share the rest of your life with.'

She ought to be feeling grateful to him that he hadn't acted as Giles would have done in the same circumstances. And she was; in a way she was. But another part of her was stirred with such a tremendous sense of loss it was making it difficult to think. She didn't understand why this man had got under her skin from the moment she'd laid eyes on him, but he had. And her response to him was cerebral as well as physical, much as she would have liked to explain her weakness away as merely sexual attraction. Everything had slotted into sharper focus since Zac had come into her world and the power of his attraction was frightening. It would have been frightening even if he had wanted her in the same way she wanted him—

The thought caused an explosive full stop. How did she want Zac? Deep in her heart, how did she want him?

The answer came with terrifying simplicity: for ever.

Stupid, stupid, stupid, she berated herself in the next instant, her hands clenched into fists under the duvet. Even without his corrosive history, someone as handsome, as striking as Zac would never be seriously interested in a woman like her. Long ago she'd faced the fact she was only average—average height, average build, average face. And she had been grateful for even that after a childhood of being the ugly duckling.

'Have I upset you? I didn't want to do that.'

His voice was deep and husky and she wished she could see his face, even as she knew she'd die if he turned the light on and read what surely must be in *her* face. Swallowing over the hard, painful lump in her throat, she whispered, 'I'm upset for you, for what you must have gone through. But I repeat, you've always been very honest with me, Zac.'

'Not really.' It was rueful, even self-derisive. 'If it's truthfulness we're majoring on here, I've wanted you from the first moment I laid eyes on you—wet, wind-blown and incredibly antagonistic to the supposed burglar ransacking your home.'

Rachel's heartbeat surged into a frantic rhythm.

'This weekend was going to be a full-on seduction to get you warm, willing and wanton in my bed.'

Bull's-eye in every regard, then. She couldn't help but

smile—it was either that or cry, and she didn't intend to shed any more tears that night.

'Rachel? Say something,' he said into the lengthening silence. 'Anything to put me out of my misery.'

Like what? 'I'm sorry the weekend hasn't turned out quite like you planned,' she said with weak sarcasm.

'So am I.' His voice exuded a low sensuality that would have made her weak at the knees if she hadn't been lying down. The tone changed as he added, 'But it needn't be wasted, need it? If I promise to behave myself, we can still have a good time.' He hesitated for only a moment. 'I like being with you, Rachel. More than I've liked being with someone for a long, long time. Do you believe that?'

Speaking from the heart in a way she wouldn't have been able to do but for the blanketing darkness, she said, 'No.'

'No?' His voice was so surprised it was almost soprano. Then in a more normal tone, he said, 'That's the wrong answer.'

'It's the honest answer and we seem to be going for honesty tonight.'

'OK. Still on that theme, why is it so unlikely I want to be with you more than any other woman?'

She might have known he'd go for the jugular. Picking her words carefully and vitally aware of the male body inches away from hers, she said, 'I'm nothing special, Zac, and you're a man who must be used to beautiful women.'

'Forgetting for the moment that beauty is only skin deep and it takes the whole woman—body, soul and spirit—to hold a man, you're one hell of a beautiful woman, Rachel. What you see when you look in the mirror is clearly different from anyone else, but take it from me, you turn men on without trying.'

Now he was being kind. And she clearly hadn't been able to make *him* lose his head or she wouldn't still be a virgin right now. Deciding the conversation needed to be steered elsewhere, she decided to state the obvious. 'From the weather reports tonight it looks like we'll be snowed in for the weekend so it would be silly not to make the best of it. So we carry on as friends?'

Even as she said it she knew she was being ridiculous. She and Zac had never been friends. From the first, something vital and electric had made that impossible, and now it was even more so. But she wanted this weekend. Dangerous as it was to play with fire, she wanted two whole days where she had him to herself. Well, herself and a pub full of warbling walkers, that was.

'Friends,' he agreed very softly, and the next moment she felt his hand find her chin and turned her face so he could kiss her lips. It was a light kiss, a mere skimming of her lips, but as he settled himself on his side of the bed once more her throat had gone dry and the burning ache of wanting that had been glowing since he had touched her fanned into fierce life. This was so unfair, all of it, she thought wretchedly.

The wind was moaning outside and the landlady had clearly turned the central heating off for the night because the temperature inside the room was getting steadily cooler. Rachel snuggled deeper under the covers, taking care not to touch the hard masculine body lying beside her. But she remembered how it had felt—warm, powerful, his arousal rigid against her belly.

She knew she wasn't going to be able to sleep for a long time.

CHAPTER EIGHT

WHEN Rachel awoke just before eight the next morning, it was with the sensation of slowly surfacing through layers of deep fog. Not surprising considering she hadn't been able to fall asleep until nearly dawn, and even then she'd slept in fits and starts, terrified of inadvertently curling up to Zac.

She hadn't been able to tell if Zac was awake during the long night hours. His breathing had certainly indicated he was asleep, being even and steady, but something had told her he was feigning it. Whatever, she had remained resolutely still physically, although her mind had more than made up for her body's lack of movement, whirling and dissecting and running riot.

For the first couple of hours she'd told herself she was mistaken, that what she felt for Zac wasn't love but sexual attraction, lust if you like, and as such easily put aside once the object of the desire was gone. And she might have been able to carry on convincing herself if they hadn't had their earlier conversation. As it was, the bitter facts about his marriage and the loss of his child had kept nagging away until she'd finally admitted to herself around two in the morning that, if things had been different, he very possibly might have been 'the one'.

That little piece of virtuous integrity kept her awake for another two hours as she played every possible scenario for the future over and over in her head. The possibilities ranged from Zac saying goodbye once the weekend was over and not contacting her again during his stay in England to him having a miraculous change of heart and falling in love with her, along with every conceivable—and inconceivable—spin-off from the two.

A good half an hour was spent dissecting whether she could trust her judgement after Giles; thirty minutes of taking apart every word Zac had said and inspecting it under the microscope. At the end of that time, she'd come to the conclusion that nothing in life was an absolute but that Zac was as different from Giles as it was possible to be and she'd been a fool not to recognise that before. Or perhaps she had. Perhaps she'd known from that initial meeting and that was why she'd been so frightened of getting involved with him. She'd known he was her Waterloo.

Because let's face it, she told herself at last, her head aching, he's utterly drop-dead gorgeous in every way, and you are a mere mortal. End of story.

This last pearl of wisdom had produced a dull weariness, making her mind and body feel heavy, and it was after that she must have drifted off to sleep. But it had been fitful.

Now the last veil of fog cleared and she opened her eyes.

'Good morning.' Zac's tawny eyes glittered like a cat's in the light coming from the skylights positioned over the bed, which were encrusted with a layer of sparkling snow. He was lying on one elbow and the sight of him, hair tousled, stubble on his chin and his hairy chest, took her breath away. At the same moment, she had the unwelcome thought that he had been watching her while she'd slept, morning face and all. Terrific.

'Good morning,' she whispered, knowing she was blushing but unable to do anything about it.

His lips spread back from white, even teeth as he smiled. 'I love it that you do that,' he murmured, touching her hot cheek with a lingering finger. 'I thought the modern woman had lost the art, but not you. I find it immensely…satisfying.'

He made it sound like an attribute rather than a weakness that made her resemble a boiled lobster. Rachel grimaced. 'I don't.' Surreptitiously checking that her top hadn't ridden up over her breasts in the night, she sat up, brushing her hair out of her eyes. She'd survived the night, then. 'What's the time?' she asked matter-of-factly, trying for normality.

'Nearly eight. I've only just woken myself.' He touched her hair, murmuring to himself, 'Beautiful, like multicoloured silk. Did you know your hair has an amazing array of shades in it when you study it? Fascinating.'

She wrinkled her small nose. 'It's dark brown.'

'Dark brown with all the different shades of autumn leaves,' he corrected softly. 'And your eyes are the colour of the wild cornflowers I used to pick as a child, just verging on violet.'

Rachel was sitting with the covers held against her chest. She knew at some point she was going to have to get out of bed in her skimpy pyjamas, and considering they'd shared a bed she shouldn't be feeling so hotly embarrassed, should she? Trying to emulate Zac's easy, insouciant manner, she forced a smile. 'I had no idea you had such a poetic streak.'

'There's nothing like sleeping together to find out those little things about someone.' His eyes were dancing.

The colour that had begun to subside rose again in a crimson flood. 'I suppose not,' she said primly, refusing to rise to the bait. 'Shouldn't we start getting ready for breakfast?'

Zac laughed and slid out of bed, stretching like a big cat. Rachel found her gaze was riveted on him, every magnificent muscled inch. The lights had been dim last night but now she could see just how lithe and tanned the beautifully honed body was. She had to tell herself to breathe.

If Zac was aware of her rapt attention, it didn't bother him. He walked to where he'd dropped his towel the night before, wrapping it round his hips and rummaging in his suitcase for fresh clothes before he stood up again as best he could in the low-ceilinged room. 'I'm happy to take the first stint in the bathroom, give you time to wake up properly,' he offered casually turning to face her again. 'OK?'

Rachel nodded, thinking she'd never been more awake in her life. Zac Lawson practically stark naked would wake the dead.

He walked across to where she sat, bent and touched her cheek. 'I can never tell what you're thinking,' he murmured softly, 'unlike most women. I find that… intriguing.'

Thanking her lucky stars that was the case because her thoughts would undoubtedly have shocked the pants off him more than once, she looked up at him. 'I was wondering what was for breakfast,' she lied, smiling. 'Riveting stuff, eh?'

He grinned, and then his smile died as their gazes

held. She closed her eyes as he kissed her with a controlled hunger that stirred her blood, and when she opened them again he was already at the bedroom door. He left the room without a backward glance, shutting the door carefully behind him as he ducked out.

Rachel stared after him for some moments and then jumped out of bed. She'd dress now and then undress for a quick wash in the bathroom, she decided. No doubt it would amuse him but that couldn't be helped—she needed all the protection she could get around Zac, and confronting him with just two pieces of thin silk between her and that fabulous body wasn't sensible. He might be able to control himself with admirable coolness but she was in danger of melting at his feet.

Excitement, swift and sharp, sent the blood singing through her veins before reality kicked in and reminded her that everything about her relationship with Zac was temporary. He didn't want love or togetherness or happy ever after, merely relationships that were mutually sexually satisfying for as long as they lasted. She had to keep reminding herself of that this weekend. This man didn't do for ever.

She flung her clothes on with feverish haste, just in case Zac decided to return for some reason or other, but it was fifteen minutes before he opened the bedroom door. He was fully dressed and carrying his towel and toiletry bag, and her heart bounced at the sight of him in black jeans and a heavy sweater a shade or two darker than his eyes.

She'd switched the TV on while he'd been gone but had sat gazing blankly at the screen most of the time, her mind taken up with thoughts of Zac showering, Zac having a shave, Zac running his hands through his hair and dabbing aftershave on his face. Now she bundled up her things off the bed and scuttled past him after a brief 'I won't be long.'

'Take all the time you need.' His voice floated after her. 'We've the whole weekend to relax and take things easy.'

Once in the bathroom, Rachel locked the door and then stood for some moments surveying herself in the mirror, trying to see what Zac said he saw. She shook her head in defeat. Admittedly she wouldn't exactly frighten little children but, that having been said, she was remarkably insignificant. Unbidden, a memory from the past flashed into her head. She was eight years old and it was her birthday, and she'd come down to breakfast to find a pile of presents waiting for her. One had been from a distant aunt and she'd gasped with delight when she'd unwrapped a cashmere scarf and hat in a soft dusky pink, the rim of the hat and the fringes of the scarf scattered with hundreds of tiny seed pearls.

Lisa and Claire had oohed and ahhed over the gift with her, and a little while later when she had carried a few of the dirty breakfast dishes through to the kitchen she had heard her mother and one of her sisters talking. Catching her name, she'd paused before pushing open the slightly ajar door.

'Of course you can have Aunty Mary's hat and scarf, darling, it would be totally wasted on Rachel,' her mother had said, not even bothering to lower her voice. 'Her plain little face under that beautiful cashmere would look simply ridiculous, I can't think why Mary sent it to her. I'd told your aunt she needed some new vests and pants or socks, something serviceable.'

Rachel stared into the mirror, seeing the eight-year-old child who had been so upset that day. It had been one of the few occasions when she'd stood up to her mother, probably why the incident—one of many of the same type—had remained at the back of her mind. She'd opened the door and slammed the dishes onto the breakfast bar, stating that the scarf and hat were hers and she had no intention of giving them to her sister. And if her mother took them, she'd shouted, she would write to her Aunty Mary and tell her what her mother had said.

The row that had followed had been bitter and acrimonious but she had kept the hat and scarf. Every time she'd worn them though she had remembered her mother's words and suffered agonies of embarrassment at what people must be thinking when they looked at her. Eventually she'd stuffed the exquisite items at the back of her wardrobe where they'd remained hidden until the day she'd packed to leave home. She'd reverted to wearing her old hat and scarf which her mother had bought in a dingy brown colour, the wool coarse and scratchy.

It had been a long, long time since she had shed any tears over her mother's treatment of her—she'd grown to accept her mother simply hadn't liked her youngest daughter when she'd still been at school, and with the acceptance had come a measure of self-protection. Now, as tears pricked the back of her eyes, she wasn't crying for the love she'd never had from her mother but for the hurt, bewildered little mouse of a child she'd been in those far-off days.

She brushed the tears away with the back of her hand, angry with herself for going down a road she'd long since marked closed in her mind. And she had done OK after all. She'd had her beloved grandma and their relationship had always been very special; some children don't have anyone. One thing was for sure, *her* children, if she had any, would know they were loved and adored regardless of their looks or intelligence.

Pulling herself together, she stripped off and had a quick shower, getting dressed again after moisturising all over. She applied just a smidgen of make-up—a dusting of eye shadow and one coat of mascara—before brushing her hair until it hung either side of her face like raw silk. If Zac really did think her hair was lovely— if—she'd wear it down this weekend. With little Miss Come-to-Bed Walker on the scene, she needed all the help she could get.

As the thought hit, she shook her head at herself. Did it really matter whether she wore her hair up or down, for goodness' sake? Zac was so far out of her league it was laughable. She knew that, but she wasn't going to dwell on it this weekend. And—the trace of a smile touched her lips—it was her sharing the room at the top of the inn with him, not the beautiful blonde.

Breakfast proved to be terrific—according to Zac. Not that Rachel disagreed. An array of different cereals and fruit was followed by the best cooked breakfast she'd ever had. The caramelised red onion sausages, tender bacon steaks, mushrooms, tomatoes, hash browns, fried onions and eggs done any way you liked were out of this world, and she discovered her almost sleepless night had given her a ravenous appetite. After she'd cleared her plate and had had two rounds of hot buttered toast, she relaxed back in her chair feeling at least two stone heavier.

'Whatever's on the agenda at Martin's place, it couldn't compete with this.' Zac grinned at her. He'd eaten twice as much as her but didn't appear to be feeling in the least over full. 'The food more than makes up for Gulliver's room.'

As he finished speaking, the blonde walker appeared at his elbow, favouring Rachel with a cursory smile before concentrating her charms on Zac. She was wearing the same jeans as the night before but her top was lower and tighter, clinging to her ample breasts like a second skin. 'We're going to have a snowball fight…' she dimpled '…and then split into two teams to see who can build the best snowman. Fancy joining us? It'll be fun.'

Oh, yeah, wanna bet? Rachel held onto the smile with considerable effort. The girl really was brazen.

'I think we were planning some fun of our own,' Zac said lazily, 'but thanks for the offer.'

'Oh.' The blonde clearly wasn't used to being turned down. Twice. But she recovered fast. She had youth on her side after all. 'Catch you later, then.'

Bring it out into the open. Make a joke of it. Once the blonde had tripped away to join her group, Rachel said drily, 'She fancies you. And I bet her room has a normal ceiling.'

He didn't prevaricate. 'No chance.' The golden eyes were deadly serious. 'I'm with you, which is exactly where I want to be, Gulliver's room and all.'

Part of her was hugely gratified, the other part asked why—when he'd so carefully pointed out there was no chance for them whatsoever—he was saying such beautiful things. It didn't make her feel good—well, it did, but not *completely*, not in an I've-been-waiting-for-this-moment-all-of-my-life way. 'Thank you,' she said flatly.

'You could have said that as though you meant it.'

She looked at him, a straight look. 'Zac, I've had no

experience in these kinds of situations,' she said baldly. 'I guess I don't know how to play the game.'

One dark eyebrow rose. 'To be perfectly truthful, this is a first for me. I promise you, I've never brought a woman away for the weekend, slept in the same bed and not made love.'

She didn't want to think about all the other women he'd had. Her tone severe, she said, 'You know what I mean.'

'You mean we should treat each other like a maiden aunt or a fusty old uncle?' He grinned at her. 'I would find that very difficult, Rachel.'

She stared at him helplessly, annoyed with herself that she never won in their verbal sparring. He was so very much the man of the world, so confident and sure of himself that he made her feel seven instead of twenty-seven. And yet last night, when he'd told her about the baby son he'd loved and lost, he had been different. It may have been dark but she had been able to sense something of the hidden Zac, the man no one was allowed to see or get near. His wife had betrayed him and their marriage had been a sham from start to finish—what had that done to a proud young man just starting out in life?

Blinking, she broke the hold of the tawny gaze by reaching out for her coffee cup and swallowing the last mouthful of now tepid liquid. It was only then she said, 'That wasn't what I meant and you know it. I just don't think it's particularly helpful for you to...' Her voice trailed away. She didn't know how to put it.

'Say I want to be with you? But I do. Very much.'

He was being deliberately awkward. She met the dancing eyes and in spite of herself had to smile. He was impossible.

A gust of laughter from the walkers as one member of the party threw a piece of toast at another, only to have it promptly returned in like manner, brought Zac rising to his feet. 'Shall we go?' he said, taking her arm with a coolly disapproving glance at the others. 'The children are getting out of hand.'

Her lips turned up again. The oldest of the party was easily Zac's age, probably a few years older. 'Are you sure you don't want to join in the snowball fight and have fun?' she teased as they left the room. 'You'd make one young woman very happy.'

He paused at the foot of the stairs, drawing her loosely into the circle of his arms. 'There's only one young woman I'd like to make happy this weekend,' he said softly, 'but unfortunately, my considerable skill and talent in the area I like to think my speciality are not viable with her. However, I fully intend to have fun, as you put it, and who knows, maybe even a snowball fight for two. OK?'

Rachel nodded, part of her acknowledging he'd taken the news of her virginity extremely well in the circumstances. Some men would have just brushed the reasons she hadn't slept with anyone aside and continued with the seduction technique; others would have sulked or even turned violent. Few would have reacted like Zac and not even tried to persuade her to change her mind.

Of course, it might be that he didn't fancy her that much anyway.

Zac kissed the top of her nose and held onto her hand as they walked up the stairs to the first floor, and for the umpteenth time that morning Rachel found herself marvelling that she was here, in this inn, with easily the most handsome and downright sexy man she'd ever seen, and that included the icons of the silver screen. And if he thought they were going to have fun this weekend, who was she to argue?

CHAPTER NINE

THEY went for a long walk in the winter wonderland outside the pub's warm confines after breakfast. According to the weathermen there had been a record fall of snow the night before and the sky looked low and heavy with more, but when they left the inn it wasn't snowing. The wood and meadows directly behind the inn had become an enchanted world and, with no sound of traffic from the blocked roads thereabouts, the silence was magical.

The frozen white landscape, silver-grey sky and bitter cold had created an alien universe, one in which the normal laws of nature seemed suspended, but when they entered the wood some two hundred yards behind the inn the sound of a woodpecker's rapping broke the stillness. The snow wasn't so deep here: the wood consisted mostly of tall, stately fir trees and their branches had become like a canopy of white far above, protecting parts of the grounds to some extent.

They walked with Rachel's arm tucked in Zac's and their bodies close—like a real couple, as Rachel put it to herself. The air was icily pure and exhilarating, although when eventually they came out on the far side of the wood into a meadow, the walking was hard and she found herself hanging onto him.

They'd talked of inconsequential things and Zac had made her laugh a lot, but twenty yards or so into the meadow he suddenly pulled her into his arms, kissing her until she was breathless. 'I've been wanting to do that all morning,' he whispered against the flushed cold skin of her cheek. 'You're addictive, do you know that?'

He kissed her again or perhaps Rachel kissed him, she wasn't sure. She just knew she needed the feel of him, the warmth of his lips and the hunger of his mouth. For a split second she wondered how she was going to feel when he went away back to Canada, but then she brushed the thought aside. She'd deal with that when she had to; for now, he was here.

They swayed together, his hands cupping her face for deeper penetration of her mouth, and she gave herself up to the thrill of it—the white, cold day, the pearly-grey sky and the sharp air part of the dizzily new sensations tumbling through her. Murmuring her name, Zac slid his hands into her thick coat and under the sweater she was wearing, running his fingers over the silky skin underneath her bra before moving up to the rounded swell of her breasts in their brief lacy cups.

She gasped, a shiver snaking through her at the touch of his hands, and immediately he adjusted her clothing and buttoned her coat, his voice rueful as he murmured, 'You're cold and no wonder. I'm sorry, Rachel, it's not the day for that kind of outdoor pursuit, is it?'

She wanted to tell him the weather had nothing at all to do with the way she was feeling, but he was kissing her again, his mouth nipping and caressing her lips in a way that took all lucid thought out of her head.

How long they stood together in the silver-white world she didn't know, but when it began to snow again it was some moments before his mouth left hers, his breathing heavy and erratic. 'You taste like honey,' he breathed against her face, and as her eyes opened to look into his, she saw the gold of his eyes was smoky dark. 'Honey laced with some kind of drug that makes me want more and more.' He released her slowly, tucking her arm through his again as he added, 'We'd better get back. According to our friendly weatherman, this is going to continue all day once it starts.'

'We haven't had our snowball fight,' she said inanely, to hide how bereft she felt now his lips had left hers.

'Later.' He smiled, his cool control in place once more. 'For now I think it's home and a hot toddy.'

Home. It was only an expression but the word pierced like a spear, suggesting an intimate cosiness that would never be.

Zac must have noticed something because as they began walking his tone was quizzical. 'What's the matter?'

'Nothing.' How could she tell him that her feelings for him had done a U-turn that both amazed and confused her? A few days ago she had been convinced she wanted nothing to do with this man and she hadn't been timid about letting him know either; now she didn't know which end of her was up. The trouble was, every minute she spent in his company, every little thing she learnt about him increased the need to be with him. And this was a no-win situation. Aware his gaze was on her, she added lightly, 'I'm torn, I guess. It's lovely to make the most of this before it turns all slushy and horrible, but at the same time a hot toddy sounds nice.'

He tucked her arm more securely in his. 'I guess the novelty of this white stuff is lost on me these days.

Canada has rather a lot in the winter.' He grinned wryly.

'I suppose so.' She glanced up at him. 'Tell me about your life, Zac. Your home, your work, your friends.' She wanted to be able to picture it when he had gone, even though it probably wasn't a good idea. 'Do you live by yourself or with your parents?'

'Hell, not my parents. Oh, don't get me wrong, they're great, but working as I do in the family firm I need my own space. After...' He hesitated for an infinitesimal moment but Rachel noticed it '...Moira died, I sold the apartment we'd been living in and rented a place for a couple of years. That was my wild time.' This pause was longer. 'And then one day I woke up in a strange bed with no recollection of the night before and realised I had to stop before I killed myself or someone else.'

The tawny eyes flashed over her face, probing, but she showed no reaction, although she was filled with pity for the lost young man he'd been then.

'So I stopped. I made my peace with my family and repented in sackcloth and ashes to my poor mother who'd been convinced she'd have to identify me on a mortuary slab one day. Then I put myself through university by taking a number of part-time jobs.'

'Your parents couldn't have supported you financially?'

'Sure.' The hard, handsome face was expressionless. 'But I needed to do it myself. When I'd got my degree, I came into the family firm and began to get some shop-floor experience—however good an academic background, you can't beat hands-on training. I bought a place a little out of town with a garden that runs down to the river, somewhere where I can fish weekends and hang out without seeing another soul if I don't want to.'

She stared at him. She'd imagined something different—a glitzy bachelor pad perhaps or an umpteen-bedroomed house where he could entertain.

'What?' He'd caught the look on her face.

'Nothing.'

'Tell me.'

She shrugged uncomfortably. She knew by now he wasn't like Giles. Giles had pretended tenderness and consideration and honesty and it had all be counterfeit, but she supposed she'd continued to liken Zac to Giles inasmuch as she'd expected him to enjoy being the centre of attention at parties and entertaining and such like. He was so handsome, so charismatic she'd imagined he'd fly with the smart set and have something of a…superficial life. But she couldn't very well say that. Her mind racing, she said lamely, 'I didn't expect you to be something of a recluse, I guess.'

He didn't laugh. Instead, he considered her words for a moment or two as they walked. Then he nodded. 'I suppose you could say I'm reclusive to some extent, at least when I feel the need to be. That being said, I'm not adverse to company on certain occasions.'

His tone had been lazy but she knew he was telling her his lifestyle certainly didn't encompass celibacy. Not that she'd thought it did. Nevertheless, she was surprised how much it hurt. Stupid, Rachel, she told herself grimly. Really stupid.

'And, of course, with my father getting older I tend to run the firm pretty much these days, and that includes travelling when the need arises, like this trip to England.' He smiled at her. 'Not that any of my other trips have yielded such an unexpected bonus as this one.'

She forced a smile in return. 'And your friends?' she persisted. 'You do have friends, I take it?'

'Yes, Rachel, I have friends,' he said gravely. 'Some married, some single and one or two in the process of getting divorces. Pretty average, wouldn't you say?'

Perhaps, but Zac Lawson was far from average and that was part of the trouble.

He continued to talk about his life in Canada as they walked back to the inn, the snow falling with picture-postcard prettiness and not at all with the ferocity of the day before. But he didn't mention girlfriends, past or present.

Not that she wanted him to, not really, Rachel told herself as she listened to his low, melodic, faint Canadian drawl, but at the same time she did. Which didn't make sense. Along with everything to do with this weekend.

They had no sooner passed the group of rather obese-looking snowmen in the pub's grounds and entered the warmly welcoming interior of the inn than they were pounced on by the blonde walker. 'Enjoy your walk?' she asked chirpily, and without giving them a chance to reply added, 'I'm Angel, by the way. My name's Angela but no one calls me that. Come and meet the rest of the gang.' She turned and indicated the rest of the party, who were gathered round the log fire and who smiled and opened up to include them, making it rude to refuse. 'We've got a couple of jugs of hot chocolate. Help yourself.'

They were a friendly lot. At the end of an hour Rachel had heard a couple of life stories, knew that the walking club had been going for three years—and growing all the time, the organiser, an intense young man with white-blond hair and acne assured her—and that every month they chose a different location to gather together for a whole weekend of walking.

'Lucky it was here this weekend,' Angel breathed meaningfully, her eyes eating up Zac before including the others as she said, 'This being such a great inn and all.'

Surprisingly, Rachel felt the edges of her mouth turn up. The girl was shameless and so overt in her intentions it was like watching a caricature of the original vamp.

Zac caught her eye and she knew he was thinking along the same lines because his eyes were bright with suppressed laughter. He stood up, holding out his hand to Rachel. 'Shall we freshen up before lunch?'

She escaped the group gratefully, and once they were alone in the hall giggled as she said, 'Do we take it Angel's one of the fallen kind?'

'Without a doubt.' He returned her smile lazily and it was there, in the hall of the inn with the sound of laughter and voices from the room they'd just left filtering through and the landlady sounding as though she was shouting at someone in the kitchen, that she realised this love wasn't the sort you were able to get over. It was the once-in-a-lifetime sort.

Fortunately Zac took her hand and they began to climb the stairs at that point because she was sure her face would have given her away if he'd continued to smile at her. As it was, she had managed to pull herself together by the time they'd scaled the second flight of steep, narrow stairs and Zac had followed her into their room.

Their boots and trousers had inevitably got caked with snow on the walk, and as Zac sat down on the edge of the bed and took off his boots, before unconcernedly unbuckling the belt of his jeans, Rachel sat down on her side with her back to him. She wasn't going to be able to do this, not spend another night in the same bed.

Pathetic it might be, and it wasn't even that she didn't trust Zac to show restraint. It was herself she feared. At the moment, he knew she was sexually attracted to him but that was all, and she'd die a thousand deaths if she betrayed how she really felt.

She heard him take off his jeans and then the sound of his suitcase opening and shutting. Half a minute later his voice came, wryly amused. 'You can look now.'

She had taken off her own boots but was still in her damp trousers. As he came to stand in front of her dressed in dry clothes, she schooled her face into a faintly quizzical expression. 'I don't know what you mean.'

'Sure you don't.' He grinned. 'Like me to help you off with those wet things?' he offered helpfully.

'I can manage perfectly well, thank you.'

'Considering we slept together last night, you're remarkably reticent this morning.' He quirked an eyebrow, still grinning.

'We slept in the same bed, that's all.'

His eyes widened innocently. 'Isn't that what I just said?'

This time she maintained a dignified silence and gave him a long look. Zac returned the stare, teasing her.

With a hauteur that wasn't altogether feigned, Rachel rummaged through her own clothes and found fresh jeans. Willing her cheeks not to burn, and failing miserably, she whipped off the damp jeans and pulled on the dry ones without looking at Zac. When she did raise her head he had turned to stare exaggeratedly in the opposite direction. In spite of herself she had to smile. 'You can look now. I'm quite decent.'

'Sure? I'm a sensitive soul with fragile sensibilities.'

'Quite sure.'

'Be it on your own head.' He turned and then gasped, pointing accusingly at her bare feet. 'Naked flesh. Cover yourself, woman, have you no sense of decorum?'

'Very funny, Zac.' She tried to frown but it was difficult.

'I have seen women partially dressed before without being overcome by my base male desires,' he said mildly. 'Even ones in bikinis, believe it or not. Some…' He paused dramatically, mocking her. 'Without any clothes at all. I'm well past the teenage years when raging hormones can take over and cause you to do something you later regret. You're quite safe, Rachel.'

So he'd regret sleeping with her, would he? Or was he referring to getting the girl pregnant who'd become his wife? 'I know I'm safe,' she said regally. 'And I don't know why we're having this ridiculous conversation.'

'It could have something to do with the fact that you make me feel like some lecherous old man.'

Startled, her eyes met his and although his voice had been coolly amused she could see no laughter in the piercing gold gaze, just the opposite. Weakly, she said, 'You're not old.'

'Thanks,' he murmured with dry sarcasm.

'No, what I meant was, of course you're not like that. I don't think of you like that.'

'How do you think of me, Rachel?'

She stared at him, her tongue feeling as though it was stuck to the roof of her mouth and panic riding high. This was so unfair—what did he want of her anyway? One minute he was telling her she could mean nothing in his life, that he intended to leave England at the end of his stay and conduct his life in exactly the same way as before, and the next he wanted her to bare her heart to him. Well, she didn't want to be in love with him and once he was out of her orbit it would be easier to pretend to herself. Hopefully. Her small chin rose. 'As a friend, as Jennie's cousin, of course. I thought you knew that.'

'That's all? Nothing more?'

Anger pumped in much-needed adrenalin. 'What do you want me to say, Zac?' she asked tightly. 'That I can't live without you? That I want to make love with you every hour of the next two weeks you're around? You've made it crystal clear how you conduct your life and what you want from a woman, and it couldn't be further from what I want. Admittedly I was still licking my wounds from Giles when I met you, which had coloured my view of the male sex to some extent, but deep down I've always known what I wanted out of life, and it includes marriage and children and the whole togetherness thing. That's just the way I'm made and I don't intend to apologise for it.'

'I'm not asking you to,' he said evenly, but the classical features could have been carved in stone so hard they'd become.

'Good, because I won't. I've often envied Jennie her carefree approach to life and love, but I know I'm not like her. I wouldn't survive one love affair after another, not emotionally. And I'm not a career-woman in the full sense of the word either. I like my job but I've never planned for it to be the be all and end all. I want, I *need* more than that.'

'I know that. It wasn't only me who made things perfectly clear last night. Remember?' he said icily. 'And I didn't want a lecture on morals this morning, OK?'

Her eyes widened at the injustice. 'How dare you?' she grated, absolutely furious. 'I haven't criticised you for the choices you've made or anyone else, come to it. I've just told you how *I* feel. If you want a woman while you're over here, have a word with sweet little Angel downstairs and I'm sure she'd be only too willing to meet your conditions.'

'Now you're being absurd,' he bit out heatedly.

'I think not.' She was so mad she could have punched him right on his gorgeous jaw. 'She's your sort of woman, after all.'

She watched him take a visible breath, but then moment by moment he regained control of his temper. He even adopted a mockingly sardonic expression, one dark eyebrow raised quizzically. 'What makes you think you know my "sort of woman"?' he drawled, his tone suggesting he was talking to a recalcitrant child.

Two could play at the cool I-don't-give-a-damn game. Her cheeks burning, Rachel called on all her considerable willpower. Schooling her face from a glare to a superior smile, she struck a nonchalant pose and ticked off on her fingers: 'Beautiful, independent, unattached, unconstrained, sexy and, above all, willing. Right so far? Shall I go on?'

Only a brief narrowing of his eyes betrayed he didn't like the way the conversation was going. 'Please do.'

'Liberated,' she continued sweetly, 'worldly wise, of course, someone who would be quite happy to share your life and your bed for a few weeks or even months until the thing fizzled out. Intelligent—you would want more than mere physical stimulation from a lover—'

'Thank you,' he put in with acidic sarcasm.

'And self-confident enough to bow out when the time came without any tears or regrets, nothing…messy.'

'And you think there are a number of these paragons

on tap, as it were?' he asked grimly. 'Just waiting to fall into my bed?'

She met the gold eyes fair and square. 'Aren't there? The business world is populated by such women these days, we live in a society where the modern woman is able to take what was once a man's world by the throat and live by her own rules. I know lots of women who have put all thoughts of a permanent relationship on hold while they cement their careers, planning to do the family thing when they approach forty, but that doesn't mean they're not up for some fun in the meantime. Jennie's a prime example. She intends to do the baby thing in another decade but not before.'

He was frowning now. 'What if a suitable man doesn't drop into her lap on cue? Or is she going to magic one up?'

'Zac, women don't necessarily need a man to have a baby these days, not if they're wealthy enough to visit a clinic.'

'You mean artificial insemination?'

She'd really shocked him, it was evident in his outraged voice. Good. Rachel surveyed him uncompromisingly. That would give him something to think about. 'Who's judging who on morals now?' she said in honeyed tones.

'Would *you* do that?' he demanded roughly.

'We're not talking about me.'

'But would you?' he persisted, as if it mattered.

She shook her head, her curtain of hair moving in soft tendrils against her flushed cheeks. 'No. My personal conviction is that a child needs a mother *and* a father where possible.'

The broad shoulders relaxed a little and he expelled a breath. 'How the hell did we get onto this anyway?'

She was determined not to give ground. Drop-dead gorgeous as he was, he had more than his fair share of arrogance at times. 'You started it.'

'Well, of course I would have,' he said mordantly. Then he smiled. 'Truce while we eat lunch?'

Did he know the power of that smile? And then she answered herself wryly, Too true he did. But she'd made her point with clogs on. She nodded. 'Fine by me.' In truth, she was starving despite the huge breakfast, probably due to the long walk in the fresh air. And the nervous energy she burnt up in Zac's company, another part of her mind suggested.

As she walked past him towards the door, she found herself swung round and into his arms. 'It might be a cliché,' he murmured, his eyes laughing now, 'but you're beautiful when you're angry.'

'You're right, it is a cliché,' she said as steadily as she could, considering the delicious smell and feel of him was all around her and causing sensations she could well have done without.

'And you're a mass of contradictions.' His eyes searched her face. 'I don't know where I am with you, Rachel Ellington.'

Her heart leapt but she warned herself against the potent charm. 'Funny, because I know exactly where I am with you.' She looked up at him and smiled before ducking out of his arms. 'I've caught a tiger by the tail,' she said over her shoulder as she opened the bedroom door and began to descend the stairs.

She heard his deep chuckle and every bit of her wanted to turn round and fling herself into his arms again.

'I'm no longer a wolf, then?' he murmured softly.

'Perhaps.' As he joined her on the landing she kept her tone light. 'Tigers, wolves, they're all dangerous.'

He chuckled again and she smiled too, but as they walked downstairs she knew she hadn't been joking.

CHAPTER TEN

LUNCH was followed by a lazy afternoon.

The walkers, Angel included, were determined to make the most of the snow and had gone outside to build a couple of igloos. Angel had tried to rope Zac in but eventually admitted defeat when he refused to budge from where he and Rachel were ensconced in two comfortable armchairs close to the roaring fire in the inn's lounge, a couple of drinks at their elbows.

It was very pleasant in the ancient old inn. A gently benign grandfather clock ticked away in one corner and the logs on the fire spluttered and crackled now and again, a perfect antidote to the gently falling snow outside the windows. Whether it was the cosiness of the afternoon or the fact he'd opened up a little to her the night before Rachel didn't know, but after they'd talked about this and that for a while, Zac began to talk about deeper issues—his marriage, the dark, dangerous time when he'd lost his way after Moira's death, other painful, bitter truths.

Rachel listened, knowing instinctively he rarely—if ever—revealed himself in this way, and in the mellow quietness she found it easy to talk too, about her cold, confusing childhood, the dawning knowledge that she was in a family but not part of it, her loneliness and fear that had accompanied her into adulthood and why her past had made the episode with Giles so devastating. And then silence enveloped them and she sat wondering if he regretted saying so much, because she did.

It was a relief when just as a cold winter twilight caused the landlady to switch on the lights, the others burst into the inn, shouting that a snow plough was busy clearing the road outside. Angel joined them, her lovely face glowing. 'The main roads are passable but the driver doesn't recommend anyone going anywhere tonight unless they have to, not with it snowing again,' she bubbled, plonking herself down in the chair next to Zac and pulling off her bulky fur-lined jacket so he could receive the full benefit of her generous cleavage. 'Looks like we're all stuck here for another night at least. Still, we wouldn't have met but for the snow and it's nice to make new friends, isn't it?' Her eyelashes fluttered ingenuously.

'Wonderful,' said Zac drily as the others joined them too. Soon it was hot toddies all round, and even the landlady came to sit awhile and join in the easy banter that went on amongst the walkers, who teased each other unmercifully most of the time.

Rachel sat quietly, content to listen to the others and watch Zac. He was the sort of man both sexes gravitated to, she thought. Not a lone wolf but definitely the alpha male. Other men wanted his approval and friendship, and women—well, women wanted something quite different. He would always cause a little stir wherever he went, and not just because of his physical attributes, which were impressive, but because of some undefinable presence that set him apart.

A slight stubble was darkening his chin, and during the afternoon while they'd talked he'd removed his sweater, rolling up the sleeves of his shirt to reveal strong, sinewy forearms. He exuded maleness—it was there in every gesture, every movement and it was spine-tinglingly sexy. How had a man like Zac Lawson ever come into her orbit and how had she imagined for one minute she wouldn't fall hopelessly and helplessly in love with him? It had been inevitable from the moment he'd smiled at her.

He glanced across at her suddenly, trapping her gaze, and she blushed, conscious she'd been staring. He smiled at her, a warm intimate smile, before someone else claimed his attention.

She was going to sleep in the same bed with him again tonight, lie next to him, hear the quiet, even sound of his breathing and know he was but a touch away. Last night had been bad enough but since then she felt she'd got to know so much more about him. Was she going to regret it for the rest of her life if they didn't make love? Or would she regret it more if they did? She didn't know any more. She only knew she'd never meet anyone like Zac ever again and soon he would be gone.

The thought produced an actual ache in her throat and she swallowed against it, willing herself to come to terms with what she knew. Zac was a love-'em-and-leave-'em man. Whether he would have been that way if his marriage hadn't gone so terribly wrong she didn't know, but that experience had been bad enough to send him severely off the rails for a couple of years and change him for ever. She had met him too late, much, much too late. Horrified, she realised she wanted to cry and fought desperately against the weakness.

She took a deep steadying breath and regained control, picking up her glass with a hand that shook slightly and finishing her drink.

One thing was for sure, if she wanted him to make love to her, the first move would have to come from her after all she'd said in the last twenty-four hours. She cast a hunted glance about the room, taking in the easy, smiling faces of the others before placing the glass carefully on the table. She didn't know what to do. For the first time in her adult life, she really didn't know what to do.

Rachel heard the mobile phone begin to ring but didn't realise it was Zac's until he fished it out of his jeans pocket. With the others chattering and laughing, she couldn't make out what was being said, but she saw his face and that was enough. When he stood up suddenly, she rose too, following him out of the room into the hall where it was quieter and listening in growing consternation as he took the call. She'd gathered the crux of it by the time the call finished and he met her concerned gaze.

'Your grandfather?' she asked softly.

He nodded. 'Another heart attack, but according to my father there's no chance he'll recover from this one. He's comfortable but my father's made it clear I need to get home as soon as possible if I want to say goodbye.'

'I'm so sorry, Zac.' She stared at him, horrified.

'So am I.' He shook his head. 'He's an awkward old cuss but larger than life, you know? And with a wicked sense of humour. The two of us have always got on all right. I'll miss him.' For a moment his face was open, vulnerable, in a way she hadn't seen before, but almost instantly the mask was back in place. 'I need to get to the hotel and pick up my things and find out when the first available flight is. Do you mind if we cut the weekend short?'

Horribly. 'No, of course not. But the weather...'

'With the roads having been cleared to some extent, I can make it back once I've retrieved the car, but if you'd rather stay here till tomorrow I can arrange for a car to pick you up.'

And miss precious moments with him that possibly would have to last her a lifetime? 'No, I'll come with you if I may.' He was already walking to the staircase and she followed him. Once in the room he flung his things together and left immediately, telling her he'd settle the bill with the landlady and then go and see if he could drive the car. If not, he'd ring for a taxi, he added. He'd meet her downstairs.

Rachel stood numbly in the room after he'd left, the suddenness of it all having frozen her senses. After a minute or so she began to pack, her movements automatic. Deal with the practical, don't think, she told herself grimly. He's got enough on his plate without you going all weepy.

Once downstairs, she found all of the men walkers had gone with Zac to help with the car, leaving only Angel and the other women sitting by the fire. The landlady was all concern, making her a cup of hot chocolate and clucking about the dangers of travelling in such weather, although, she added, she'd do the same thing in the same situation. 'He'd never forgive himself if he didn't try, would he?' she said soberly. 'Family is family after all, and blood's thicker than water.'

Rachel drank the chocolate and just nodded or shook her head now and again when required as the others talked. It was incredibly, shamefully selfish in the circumstances, but all she could think about was the two weeks they wouldn't have together now. She was sorry about Zac's grandfather, of course she was, but the thought of saying goodbye to him for good was killing her. Useless to tell herself you couldn't fall in love with someone you'd only known for a few days. You could and she had. Completely and irrevocably.

The walkers returned, garrulous with triumph as they described how they'd worked as a team to get the car out of the ditch and back on the road, and then Zac walked in, tall, dark and sombre. When the goodbyes were being said, Rachel noticed Angel slip a piece of paper into Zac's coat pocket—presumably with her name and telephone number written on it—but she was past caring about the blonde girl.

The whirling snow of the afternoon had given way to just the odd lazy snowflake blowing in the wind when they stepped outside. Zac took her arm as he led her over to the Aston Martin, which looked none the worse for its night in the ditch. He opened the passenger door and helped her into the car before walking round the bonnet and sliding into the driving seat.

Everyone had gathered on the doorstep of the inn to wave them off—for all the world like a couple going off on honeymoon after their wedding reception, Rachel tortured herself. And then the inn was behind them and they were on their way.

'I'm sorry about this,' Zac said as they picked up speed, but it was perfunctory. His mind was clearly already with his grandfather.

'It's fine.' Rachel had to fight against the need to touch him. 'I just hope things aren't as bad as you think.'

'He's dying, Rachel.' His voice was flat, expression-less, the same tone he'd used when he'd told her about his baby son. She wondered if he always went into close-down when he felt vulnerable, but said nothing more. If that helped him deal with this and cope with the stress involved in getting to his grandfather in time to say goodbye, so be it.

The journey wasn't as hazardous as she'd expected. The main roads were relatively clear, although great banks of snow sat on either side of the highways and there were still abandoned cars scattered here and there in lay-bys or at the edge of verges or kerbs. The nearer she got to the flat, the more Rachel prayed she wouldn't disgrace herself completely when Zac said goodbye. She'd always known it was going to happen. It had just transpired earlier than expected, that was all.

He'd driven silently for the most part, making the odd comment now and again but nothing that could be called conversation. She supposed there was nothing *to* say, after all. She was just a girl who'd featured briefly in his busy life for a few days. If he remembered her at all once he was back home, it would only be as the one he *hadn't* slept with. Which was something.

When they reached the mews it was to find it still blocked with snow. Someone had cleared a path on the pavement just wide enough to walk down but that was all. Zac parked at the top of the road and turned off the engine. 'I'll walk you to the door. That path looks pretty icy to me.'

'No need.' She really didn't want to say goodbye with Jennie and Susan liable to whisk open the door. 'Unless you want to come in and say goodbye to Jennie?' she added, as the thought hit. 'She might be in.'

He shook his head. 'I want to sort out a flight; I'll ring Jennie later.' Something of his urgency left him as it seemed to dawn on him they were parting. 'I don't want to leave you,' he murmured softly, 'not like this.'

'It's all right.' She was amazed she sounded so normal

when she was screaming inside. 'You were going to have to go sooner or later anyway, we both knew that.'

'I'll miss you.' He leant over and kissed her mouth. It had clearly been intended as a quick caress but the moment their lips touched, last night's desire flared again, hot and strong. With a groan he pulled her closer, the kiss deepening as he held her against him, his fingers moving to tangle in the silk of her hair.

His mouth was heated, demanding, and she met him kiss for kiss, half-mad with the knowledge she was losing him. No one had ever made her feel like Zac did and she knew no one would ever again, but there was no chance of a future for them. Even if he had stayed the two weeks—even if he'd stayed two months and she'd shared his bed—one day she would be exactly where she was now, saying goodbye. To give him his due, he had been absolutely straight with her. She had no one to blame for the way she was feeling but herself.

A car passing sent a flash of light into the interior of the Aston Martin and it was enough to cause Zac to freeze for a moment and then lift his head. The golden eyes held hers for a second, the pupils dilated, before he slid back fully into his seat. He drew in a deep breath, raking a hand through his hair. 'It's been years since I necked in a car with a girl,' he said wryly, his mouth twisting in a self-deprecating quirk. 'But like I've said before, you're addictive.'

Not addictive enough. Rachel attempted a smile and hoped it came off. 'I need my case from the boot and then you'd better see about booking that flight,' she murmured, to make it easy for him. 'I hope the weather doesn't delay things too much.'

Zac opened his door and extracted her case, but when she joined him on the pavement and held out her hand for it, he merely tucked it through his arm. 'I'm seeing you to the door. If you break your ankle from here to your doorstep, I'd never forgive myself and I don't think Jennie would forgive me either.'

A broken ankle was the least of her worries.

Once outside the house, Rachel looked up into his extraordinarily beautiful eyes and said with barely a tremble, 'Goodbye, Zac. It's been nice, and I hope your grandfather does recover against all the odds.'

He'd set the case down on the pavement and taken her in his arms again. Now his brows drew together. 'That sounds final. Us, I mean. I thought we could keep in touch. Phone, write, maybe? And I might be over here in the future on business again.'

Please don't do this to me. 'I don't think that's a good idea.' This had to be final for her to survive emotionally.

'Why? Because of this Giles character?'

Was he mad? She shook her head. 'It's got nothing to do with Giles,' she said carefully. 'But you're in Canada and I'm here, surely that's enough.'

'That prevents calls and letters? Come on, Rachel, it's the twenty-first century. Great silver birds fly in the sky and cut down the miles amazingly.' He paused. 'I though we were getting on OK? Have I misread the signals?'

She tried to bring her chaotic thoughts into order. 'Zac, when we talked last night we both agreed...' She took a deep breath. 'I thought we'd agreed we're very different people, that we see things differently. Your life-style isn't one I could embrace, and vice versa.' Surely he had considered they were incompatible? And that being the case, why continue the sweet torture of seeing each other, knowing it could only end messily, something he'd spent most of his adult life avoiding?

His eyes were unfathomable as they gazed into hers. 'So you don't want to keep in touch, to see me again?'

Maybe if he hadn't told her about Moira and his son she could just have said no and that would have been that. She could have walked away with her dignity intact. But he *had* told her and that had changed things. It was important he understood now because she wasn't another Moira who'd play fast and loose, but neither could she go into a relationship with him knowing it would mean little beyond a warm, willing body in bed as far as he was concerned. And at least she wouldn't see him after she'd told him.

Rachel took a deep breath and hoped his coat was thick enough so he couldn't feel her hands, which were around his waist, trembling.

'It's not that I don't want to see you again. I do. Which is why I can't.' She wasn't putting this very well, she could tell from the look on his face. 'What I mean is, I—I like you, Zac. Too much.'

His brow wrinkled. 'How can you like me too much?'

For such a worldly-wise individual, he could be incredibly dim. 'You'd break my heart when you left,' she said simply. 'As, of course, I know you would. I—I wouldn't want you for a week or a month or a year, Zac. However long it lasted before you moved on. I'd want you for ever.'

He retreated. Emotionally and physically. She saw the withdrawal in his face even as his arms dropped from around her and he took a step backwards, thrusting his hands in the pockets of his black overcoat. 'That's crazy. A few days ago I had to force you to go out to dinner with me and now you're saying you'd want me for ever?'

'I do want you for ever, that's what love does.' There, she'd said it, the word guaranteed to send him back to Canada as fast as the speed of light. 'I'm just being honest here, Zac.'

His eyes narrowed, shutting out all expression. 'You don't love me, Rachel,' he said quietly after a painful moment had dragged by. 'This is just a rebound thing after the Giles bozo. I've wined and dined you and made you feel like a woman again, and you're mistaking gratitude and attraction for something else.'

Gratitude? She might have known he'd say something to make her angry, he usually did. 'Believe me, Zac,' she said heatedly, 'gratitude is the last thing I feel towards you. You bulldozed your way into my life and turned it upside down and then made me fall in love with the most unsuitable man I've ever met. You live on the other side of the world but it might as well be on another planet so different are our lifestyles and what we want out of life. You've been totally unfair and typically male, and if I didn't love you, I'd hate you. Now I've got to try and pick up the pieces again and you calmly suggest we keep in touch so you can swan in and out of my life and make things a hundred times more difficult. No, it's definitely not gratitude I feel.' She glared at him, furious he'd made her say all that and spoil their last meeting.

'You've got to go.' From somewhere she found the strength to take control again and speak calmly. 'Go and book your flight, Zac. Every minute probably counts.'

The strength held long enough for her to stand on tiptoe and kiss his cheek, every part of her breathing in the smell and feel of him for the last time.

She was conscious he was standing like a block of granite, his face dark and grim, but she didn't intend to prolong this a second longer because she knew her control was only skin deep. Another moment and she'd fling herself at him and recant everything she'd said. And she couldn't do that, for both their sakes but especially—and she didn't apologise to herself for it either—her own.

She opened the front door and slipped inside the flat, leaving him standing there. When she shut the door, he hadn't moved. She leant against it, praying without hope he'd knock in a moment or two. He didn't.

After what seemed a long time, she crept into the sitting room and stealthily peered out of the window. He had gone. Walking through to the hall again, she opened the front door and looked to where the Aston Martin had stood. It, too, had gone.

And it was only then she allowed herself the luxury of tears.

CHAPTER ELEVEN

'Oh, *Rachel*. Why didn't you say you'd keep in touch? You might wear him down that way. You know, the steady drip, drip.'

It was two in the morning and Jennie and Susan had returned from a night on the town a little while earlier to find Rachel still crying. After making a pot of coffee, her two friends had settled down with tissues and comfort and listened to the whole story, patting her hand or giving her a hug at the appropriate moments and saying all the right things.

Rachel turned pink-rimmed eyes on Jennie. 'I don't want to wear him down, that's why. He is as he is and if he couldn't enter wholeheartedly into a relationship, it's never going to work. I wouldn't want to be wondering every minute when it's going to end. I'm not made that way.'

'But if you'd carried on with him, he might have begun to think he couldn't do without you.'

Rachel shook her head wearily. 'Jen, be real. We're talking Zac Lawson here. Why would he believe he couldn't do without me? Women queue to be the next in his bed, for goodness' sake.'

'Did he say that?' Jennie asked indignantly.

'He didn't have to. You ought to have seen that little

blonde at the inn I told you about. She was practically salivating every time she looked at him. She was
young and cute and up for it, believe me. And the sort
of women he comes into contact with all the while—
sophisticated, experienced career types—are going to
be just like Angel but more blasé in their approach.' She
gazed pitifully at her friends and they both put their
arms round her.

'It's a bummer,' Susan muttered in her ear.

'In a word.' She nodded. 'So that was why it's no
contact. Why prolong the agony? All pain and no gain.
And I'd end up a head case. Well, more of a head case
than I am already.'

'Of course, if you slept with him you could always get
yourself accidentally pregnant,' Jennie said thoughtfully,
'If you're sure he is the one, of course.'

'Jennie!' Two pairs of shocked eyes stared at Zac's
cousin.

'What?' Jennie wasn't the least concerned by their
condemnation. 'The best scenario is that he might realise what he's been missing all these years—a wife and
a family—and ask you to marry him and it's happy ever
after; the worst, you have the baby and not only is that
always a link with him but you've got a little piece of
Zac to love. I'm sure he'd provide for the mother of his
child.'

'I couldn't possibly do that.' Rachel hadn't revealed
Zac's history and had no intention of doing so. Somehow
she knew he'd hate that. 'It would be trapping him in
the worse possible way.'

'I couldn't agree more.' Susan glared at Jennie.

Jennie shrugged. 'In your place I'd do it.'

'Which says it all.' Susan shook her head helplessly.
'You really are the pits at times, Jen.'

Jennie grinned, not in the least offended. 'So hey, who said I was perfect? But one thing's for sure, I won't end up with a broken heart. A girl needs to be one step in front these days.'

She had a point. Rachel blew her nose and sat up straighter. She could never do what Jennie was suggesting, but this wasn't going to crush her either. She would get through. Albeit with broken fingernails as she clung on like grim death. But she was not going to crumble.

Rachel had to remind herself of that countless times over the next days. Knowing he'd gone for good was harder than she'd expected.

She came home from work on the Monday evening to find Zac had left a message on the answering machine, ostensibly for Jennie. He was sorry to have left so suddenly without thanking her for her hospitality but, as he was sure Rachel would have explained, it had been unavoidable. He'd had a short time with his grandfather before he'd passed away, for which he was thankful, but now, of course, there were funeral arrangements and things of that nature. He wished them all a merry Christmas and happy new year.

Rachel played the message ten times and then deleted it. The temptation to keep it and hear his voice was too much. Zac was back in his world, a world she could never inhabit, and once he'd come to terms with his grandfather's death, life would go on as normal. And she had to pick up the pieces here and get on with it.

She hadn't slept much the night before but she slept even less that night. It was one thing knowing you were doing the only thing you could for self-survival, and quite another hearing his voice. But she woke up in the morning, admittedly bleary-eyed and working on automatic, and got through the day.

The weather turned milder. The snow turned to slush and then disappeared altogether as December progressed. She was called into the office of the great 'I am' and told she had the manager's position when Jeff transferred after Christmas. They were very pleased with her progress to date apparently, and she was greatly valued for who and what she was.

Rachel contemplated asking the managing director, a rosy-faced individual with a receding hairline and thin lips, if he could let her in on the secret of who she was, but decided against it. The managing director wasn't noted for his sense of humour. But she was pleased about the promotion. If nothing else, it would provide a focus in the coming year.

She celebrated that weekend with an impromptu party for which all her friends and colleagues turned out. The flat was filled to overflowing and everyone drank too much. It was around three in the morning she found herself in the bathroom, cold, stone sober and looking down the years in front of her with something approaching horror. If only she could go to sleep and never have to wake up again, she thought. Never have to wake up to a world in which Zac didn't feature.

The negative power of the thought was enough to jerk her out of the maelstrom of self-pity, and once everyone had gone—the last stragglers disappearing as a mother-of-pearl sky heralded a cold winter dawn—she fell into bed and slept until midday.

She awoke before Jennie and Susan and, after making herself a cup of coffee, curled up on the sofa in the sitting room, the debris of the party all around her.

She had to get some truths straight in her mind. She

inhaled the fragrant aroma rising from the mug in her hands, her gaze inward looking. She could never be more than a passing pleasure in Zac's life if she contacted him, as she ached to do. One of many females who had briefly brightened his nights and featured superficially for a short time in his life. And she couldn't be like that. She loved him.

She twisted restlessly, wondering what he was doing right at this moment. The funeral was over, he had texted Jennie to say it had gone as well as these things ever went. He would have picked up the threads of his life in Canada by now; he might even be looking forward to the family Christmas he'd talked about, although of course it would be bitter-sweet with his grandfather's death so recent. But Zac was rational and logical: that razor-sharp, clear mind would have determined it was time to move on.

Tears flooded into her eyes and rolled down her face. If only she could do the same. But she would, she would.

She gulped at the coffee, scalding hot though it was. She had to, even though she knew her love for him was not a passing fancy. She loved him with an intensity that had never been there with Giles, could never be there with anyone else. He was…Zac. Flawed maybe, difficult certainly, but perfect nonetheless.

Rachel stretched, but the ache in her chest was emotional, not physical. It was her heart that was being squeezed dry.

He would never understand that it was because she loved him she couldn't cope with a temporary relationship. To him commitment meant vulnerability and pain, something that would suck the life out of him and grip him in a stranglehold. But she admitted it, she was greedy. Greedy for a total life with him, the loving, the good and bad times, all of it.

Impossible relationship. Whatever way you looked at it, impossible. Some things were meant to be and others weren't…

She finished the coffee and had a shower before dressing quickly. She ought to start clearing up the mess left after the party and she would, but not right now. She needed to get out into the fresh air and walk, it didn't matter where. Anywhere would do. She needed to be one of the anonymous masses.

She walked for two hours and when she got back to the flat Jennie and Susan were still fast asleep. By the time they roused themselves, she had cleared up after the party and put the flat to rights and was sitting reading the papers she had bought on her walk while their meal cooked in the oven. Normal Sunday. Except nothing was normal any more.

Five days before Christmas, Rachel did battle with her mother on the telephone. Her mother was determined that this year her errant daughter would come home for Christmas, and Rachel was equally determined she wouldn't. She had nothing in common with her mother and sisters, she never had had, but most of her mother's friends had big family gatherings and Anne Ellington was clearly feeling it looked bad that Rachel didn't return to the nest. Reading between the lines, Rachel was sure someone had said something and her mother had taken umbrage.

'You haven't even seen your latest nephew.' Her mother's voice was icy with condemnation. 'And sending a card and present when he was born is hardly adequate.'

'He's two months old, Mother. He's hardly going to know if his Aunty Rachel is there or not.'

'That's not the point and you know it. I insist you come, Rachel.' There was a pause and then in true Machiavellian style her mother continued, 'You can bring that young man of yours if you want. There's the spare room, as you know.'

Very clever, Mother. Don't ask straight out if we're still together because that would show you're curious, and you've spent a lifetime of showing me you don't care. 'I'm sorry, but I've made other arrangements. Jennie's parents are expecting me.'

'You can cancel *them*.' It was scathing. 'Ring them.'

'I'm sorry but I can't do that, not at this late date.'

There was a longer pause and then her mother's voice became low and deadly. 'You amaze me, girl. You've got no pride, have you? Forcing yourself on Jennie's family or Susan's year after year, they must wince at the sound of your name.'

The familiar curdling in the pit of her stomach that her mother's venom always produced made itself felt. For the first time in her life, however, Rachel didn't feel the need to defend herself or argue. Losing Zac was the worst that could have happened, her mother's spitefulness was nothing in comparison. Calmly, she said, 'Goodbye, Mother,' and put down the phone.

It rang again immediately and she let it go to the answering machine. 'How *dare* you hang up on me, girl? How dare you? You answer me right now or, by heaven, I tell you, Rachel, I've only got two daughters. I mean it, girl, do you hear me? You always were an insolent, unpleasant child and you've grown into a sour young woman with nothing to commend her. I *order* you to pick up the phone.' The tirade lasted until the machine cut her off.

The room swelled with a heavy silence as she sat looking at the telephone, and for the life of her she didn't know whether to laugh or cry because it was the finish, she felt it in her bones. She did neither. Rising from the chair where she'd sat to answer the telephone having just come in from work, she walked through to the kitchen where she poured herself a glass of wine. Raising it in a toast, she said, 'Happy Christmas, Mother,' and set about preparing dinner. It wasn't until Jennie and Susan came home that she even realised her cheeks were wet.

Four days before Christmas she met Jennie and Susan after work and the three of them did their Christmas shopping in one huge spree. Most of the shops stayed open until after ten o'clock to catch the Christmas trade, and by the time they got home and then ordered in a couple of pizzas while they sorted out their packages, it was nearly midnight. She flopped into bed that night too tired to think, but long before it was light she was awake and thinking about Zac, wondering what he was doing, who he was with. Especially who he was with.

He hadn't tried to contact her. The shaft of pain was so acute she flinched, even as she reminded herself he was doing exactly what she'd told him she wanted. And if nothing else, it proved she'd been absolutely right to finish it cleanly and decisively. If there had been a glimmer of something more than sexual attraction in his feelings for her, he would have made some attempt to see if she was all right, if nothing else. He could do without her very easily and it would have been emotional suicide to continue hanging on. She believed that—in her head. It was just her heart that was having trouble accepting it.

Three days until Christmas. Her heart sank. If it wasn't for the fact she knew Jennie wouldn't let her, she'd have stayed at the flat alone this year. She didn't want to spoil anyone else's Christmas and so she knew she would have to force a gaiety she didn't feel all over the festive period. Jennie's parents had moved to a huge, sprawling cottage in Kent a few years ago and still had an unmarried son and daughter living with them, although three older sons were married with families. Everyone descended on Jennie's parents on Christmas Eve and stayed over until Boxing Day or longer if they could, so the old house groaned at the seams and there was no nook or cranny for any private moments. Which was fine—normally.

Today it was the firm's Christmas drinks party in the afternoon when everyone would be very jolly and upbeat, pretending to have a good time even though myriad office politics would be simmering under the surface. Rachel shook her head at herself. She was getting grouchy, she'd have to watch that. If she wasn't careful, she'd end up a crabby old spinster whom nobody liked, living alone with just a cat for company. Except she didn't particularly like cats.

She dressed with more care than normal that day with the Christmas party in mind, her silk-mix white top with silver edging and smart white trousers teamed with silver boots and bag, all new and bought for Christmas Day at Jennie's parents' house when everyone dressed up.

As the firm provided 'nibbles' in generous quantities, no one bothered with lunch, and Rachel and a couple of colleagues were standing with plates full of deliciously filled vol au vents and tiny cream cheese and bacon baked potatoes as they chatted with a group of clients when someone hovering on the perimeter of her vision caused her to turn her head.

Giles. For a moment she couldn't believe he'd had the audacity to come, but the next moment she thought, Why not? That was Giles all over, shameless. When Melanie had come to see her and she'd told him exactly what she thought of him there had been no remorse, only regret he'd been found out.

She turned back to the others and continued the conversation as though her heart wasn't thudding like a sledgehammer, but once the group dispersed and she moved on to talk to other clients, as the firm expected their employees to do, Giles was at her elbow.

'Rachel.' His voice was as smooth and carefully seductive as she remembered. 'I've been longing for this moment. I only came today to see you.'

'Hello, Giles.' She didn't smile and *her* voice had all the warmth of an arctic winter. 'How are you?'

'Still bereft at losing you.'

She stared at him, amazed that even Giles would dare to take such a tack, and the pale blue eyes with their blond lashes smiled confidently back at her. For the first time she saw the emptiness in those eyes and the weakness in the mouth she'd once thought so attractive. She must have been blind before.

'I suppose you've heard Melanie and I are no longer together?' he said softly. 'It's been a little while now.'

Rachel shook her head, assailed with so many feelings she couldn't name them except one—self-disgust that she'd ever got involved with this man. He was as different from Zac as chalk to cheese—how could she have imagined for one moment that she cared for him? Actually contemplated *marrying* him?

'She met someone.' He couldn't quite hide the amazement that his wife could prefer another man to him.

'She left you?' Well, good on you, Melanie. The worm had finally turned and she couldn't be more pleased.

He nodded, flicking back the quiff that fell over his forehead. 'In the autumn. Of course, the marriage was never right to begin with. Melanie was so difficult and possessive.' He did the wistful little-boy look that had once charmed her but now made her feel slightly sick as he said, 'I never got over you, I guess that was partly the trouble. Can I take you out to dinner, Rachel? Please? I need to tell you how sorry I am.'

When hell froze over. 'You've told me, Giles.'

'Not properly.' He moved closer. 'We had something good, didn't we? And I know you loved me. We can be like that again, but it will be better this time. I can give you all of me.'

Ugh, over her dead body.

Her face must have spoken for itself because his changed, the winsome smile disappearing. 'I know you're still hurt and angry and I can understand that, but give me a chance to make it up to you. Please, Rachel. I wanted to tell you about Melanie, I swear it, but I was terrified of losing you.'

In the first devastating days after Melanie had come to see her, she had imagined Giles coming crawling one day and the satisfaction she'd feel when she sent him packing. Funnily enough, all she felt now was an overwhelming sense of relief she was rid of this man. Quietly, aware of the odd surreptitious glance her way from colleagues who knew what had happened, she said,

'I'm not hurt or angry, Giles. That only lasted a short time. I've moved on, that's all.'

As she turned to move away he swung her back with a hard hand at her elbow. 'What's his name?' he hissed.

'I beg your pardon?' Aware of where they were, she couldn't do what she wanted to do, which was probably a good thing. She'd never indulged in physical violence before. As it was, she jerked her arm free and glared at him. 'Don't touch me, Giles.'

'There's someone else, isn't there?'

It was for all the world as though he was the injured party. Freshly amazed at the sheer cheek of him, she took a moment to calm down before she said, 'If you're asking if I'm in love with the most fabulous man on the planet, the answer's yes. But even before I met him I was well and truly over you, Giles. It didn't take long. Now, please leave me alone.'

'You little—'

As Giles went to reach out to her again, one of her colleagues—a six-foot-four rugby player with a body like a barn door—grasped his wrist none too gently. Liam was a devoted family man with two children and a dog, and he'd been outraged on her behalf when the truth about Giles had become known. Now he smiled pleasantly as he said, 'If you're not out of here in two minutes flat, I'll take great pleasure in kicking your butt all the way down the stairs. OK?' He placed Giles's arm by his side, patting his suit jacket and continuing to smile into the pale face, which had gone a shade paler. Giles was clearly scared to death.

'How—how dare you? I'm a client here, I pay your wages.'

Liam cut across the spluttering by the simple expedient of glancing at his watch. 'Thirty seconds gone already. Goodbye, Mr Hammond. And merry Christmas.'

For a moment Rachel thought Giles was going to protest further, but after a furious glare at them both, he marched across the room and disappeared out of the door. Her body relaxed and she breathed out shakily. Liam grabbed a glass of wine from a passing waiter and handed it to her. 'The second option would have been more fun,' he murmured with a sly grin.

She smiled. 'Not if we'd both ended up getting the sack.'

'True.' He indicated the glass. 'Drink, it'll soothe the jangled nerves. And I don't think that creep will be back.'

'Thanks, Liam. Not for the wine, for stepping in when needed.' She shook her head. 'I can't believe I was stupid enough to get mixed up with him and believe he was on the level.'

'It happens to the best of us, and while we're on the subject, I'd just like you to know that none of us here knew he was married when you started seeing him. We'd have told you if we'd known because you're not that type of girl, we're all aware of that.'

Touched, she patted the big, brawny arm under the smart suit. 'Thanks again.' People could be so nice. Now, if Zac could just walk in the door and take her in his arms and tell her he had realised he couldn't do without her, this little scenario would be rounded off nicely.

He didn't, of course.

CHAPTER TWELVE

ON CHRISTMAS EVE the cold weather from the north, which had blown in over the last days, promised snow. When Rachel awoke that morning she stretched lazily, glancing across at Jennie who was still buried under her covers like a dormouse. They'd both broken up for the holidays the day before and intended to travel to Kent later that morning in Jennie's trusty little Fiesta, which was ancient but which ran like a dream.

Climbing out of bed and padding across to the window, Rachel drew back the curtains and peered out, to the accompaniment of loud snores from Susan's room. Fleeting wisps of silver tinged the grey-white winter sky and at the end of the mews the main road was already jammed with traffic.

Susan and Henry were flying to Edinburgh just before lunch to spend Christmas with Susan's family, and Rachel and Jennie fully expected her to come back engaged to Henry. Jennie had just applied for a job at a different fashion house and gained an interview after Christmas. If she succeeded in securing the post, it would mean she would be travelling three weeks out of every four and rarely be home.

Everything was changing.

Rachel sat looking out for some time, her heart aching

and her mind grappling with what the new year was sure to bring. Hard work mostly, she told herself wryly. She needed to prove she could do the manager's job from day one and that meant long hours and total commitment. But she didn't mind that. If nothing else, work would be a welcome panacea for the emptiness of her personal life.

Unbidden, Zac suddenly thrust himself onto the screen of her mind. She closed her eyes as her heart lurched and then raced.

He'd be involved in that big family Christmas he'd described to her. What had he said? 'Christmas is a time for being where the heart is.' Would he think of her at all? Or had he already found someone else? Someone who was prepared to meet him on his terms? A succession of beautiful women joined the picture.

Ten minutes of brooding later, she suddenly jumped up, angry and irritated with herself for doing exactly what she'd determined she wouldn't do from now on. Someone or other, Confucius perhaps, had said you had to accept what you couldn't change. Mind you, that Chinese philosopher of two and a half thousand years ago hadn't fallen in love with Zac Lawson.

Walking through to the kitchen, she made a pot of coffee and had just sat down with a mug when Jennie and Susan joined her. They had breakfast and opened the post, which was mainly a few last-minute Christmas cards, and once dressed began to load Jennie's car with brightly wrapped packages and their cases and bags. Henry arrived for Susan at half-past nine and after waving the two off in a taxi to the airport, Rachel and Jennie had another coffee before setting off themselves.

The traffic was pretty horrendous in the city but

eventually, after waiting in one traffic jam after another, they were clear of inner London and properly on their way. The journey was mostly on A roads, and although it was bitterly cold and overcast, the first flakes of wispy, lazy snow didn't begin to fall until after they'd stopped for lunch at a nice little oak and brass pub and were on their way again.

Rachel was a bit worried about Jennie. Her friend had been perfectly all right while she'd eaten her steak and ale pie and veg, followed by a large helping of strawberry cheesecake, but then they'd gone to the ladies before leaving and she'd had to wait ages for Jennie in the little lobby the toilets led off. When Jennie had eventually emerged she hadn't seemed herself at all.

'What's the matter?' She'd taken one look at Jennie's face and suspected the worse. 'Have you got a tummy upset?'

'No. Yes.' Jennie seemed unable to make up her mind. 'I mean, possibly. I don't feel quite…right.'

'Do you want me to drive?'

'No, no, I'm OK for driving. I'll tell you if that changes.'

'I used to have a Fiesta when I was at uni, don't forget, so I'm used to them, even though I haven't driven for a couple of years.' When she had sold her last car she hadn't bothered to get another, deciding it was more hassle than it was worth and tubes and trains were so handy. Jennie, on the other hand, regularly popped home to see one or another of her large family and loved having her own transport. 'Don't soldier on if you feel unwell,' she added with another worried glance at her friend as they had exited the pub and Jennie got into the driver's seat of the car.

After they had been on the road for half an hour and

Jennie hadn't spoken once, Rachel knew she must be feeling ill. In the nine years or so since she'd known Jennie, she couldn't ever recall her friend being silent for more than five minutes unless she was asleep, and even then she sometimes nattered away six to the dozen in an unintelligible gabble.

It began to snow more heavily, fat feathery flakes that immediately settled on the frozen ground and turned the verges at the side of the road white.

By the time they came to Tenterden and had only another ten miles or so to travel until they reached the pretty little village where Jennie's parents lived, Rachel was convinced Jennie was on the verge of collapsing. If she'd asked Jennie once she had asked her a dozen times if she was all right, and the answer had always been the same. 'Fine, don't fuss. Let me drive in peace.'

The windscreen wipers were labouring to clear the snow now, and although it was only mid-afternoon it seemed much later. Since Tenterden they'd been travelling on a B road, passing small country towns and villages where Christmas tree lights in the windows of houses lit the snowy scene with a touch of magic in the darkening afternoon.

Rachel didn't trouble herself to try and make conversation any more, she was lost in heart-wrenching, painful memories of that other snowy day nearly three weeks ago. That blizzard had been the means of her getting to know Zac more intimately than he would have liked; thinking back, she was sure he wouldn't have revealed so much but for the unusual circumstances. He probably resented the fact he'd let his guard down and talked about his baby son and failed marriage. He'd want to brush that under the carpet now and forget he'd ever known an unremarkable English girl who was as dull as ditchwater compared to the glitzy, dazzling women who normally featured in his life.

She was so immersed in her thoughts that she didn't realise they'd pulled into Jennie's parents' drive until Jennie cut the engine with a deep sigh. 'Whew. I wouldn't want to do that every day. I can enjoy the snow now I don't have to drive in it, though.'

'You were great.' She had been. But that was Jennie all over. She wouldn't let anything like a snowstorm stop her from getting where she wanted to be, however she was feeling. 'Now tell me honestly, how do you feel?'

Instead of answering her, Jennie pulled open her door. 'Stay put. I'll get Dad and some of the others to help carry everything inside. Just tell them which things are breakable, would you?' And before Rachel could answer, she'd shut the door again and hurried off, leaving Rachel staring after her in surprise.

Rachel watched her friend leave deep imprints in the snow as she walked up to the front door and knocked. The door opened, she caught a brief glimpse of light and colour and then it closed again. And remained closed as the minutes ticked by.

Charming. Rachel looked out at the whirling snow and then the cottage. All the curtains were closed and the glow from within seemed to accentuate that she was sitting out here alone. Her mother's words—which she hadn't repeated to a soul—flashed through her mind. 'Forcing yourself on Jennie's family or Susan's year after year, they must wince at the sound of your name.' Perhaps her mother had been right after all.

If it had been within her power at that precise moment to transport herself somewhere else—anywhere else— she would have done so. Mortified at the realisation that she was within a moment of making a complete fool of herself by breaking down, she closed her eyes tightly and fought against tears with every fibre of her being, hating the self-pity.

She didn't hear the front door open again. The first she knew that someone was at the car was when the driver's door was pulled open and a big body slid inside.

'Hallo, Rachel,' Zac said very softly.

Rachel's hands flew to her mouth. She blinked, but he was still there. This definitely wasn't Jennie's dad. Not unless she had finally flipped and lost it completely. 'You—you're in Canada,' she muttered through her fingers.

'Why would I be in Canada when you're here?' He reached out and moved her hands from her mouth, kissing her until they were both trembling.

'No.' From somewhere she found the strength to draw back, her eyes betraying her wild hope and confusion. 'You left. You—you don't want me, not in the same way I want you.'

'If you want me so much that you can't sleep or eat or think, that every day is a lifetime and every night is an eternity, then I want you in the same way.'

'No.' With a despairing sigh, she shook her head. 'You said commitment is a route you'll never go down. You said—'

'I said a lot of things, my love, except what was in my heart.' Bending his head, he captured her mouth again, his lips firm and gentle and so, so persuasive. When he broke the contact it was to cup her face in his big hands. 'Listen to me, honey, because I mean every word I'm saying. From the first moment I laid eyes on you, I knew.' His mouth quirked. 'I saw you and it was as instant as that, and I don't care what the so-called experts might say about love at first sight being impossible.

I knew. I knew you were the woman who would turn my life upside down and it frightened me to death because I wasn't ready for it. Maybe I'd never have been ready, I don't know, but it happened and I can't go back to how things were. I don't *want* to go back to how things were. I've met you and I can't let you go.'

'But—'

'What?' He stared into her confused blue eyes.

'You could have anyone.'

'I don't want anyone, I want you. And at first, when you were so hostile, I felt relief, because it takes two. And you transparently didn't want to know. But I couldn't let it alone—I couldn't let *you* alone. I told myself it was just a sexual thing.' His voice gentled. 'But I've felt those before and this was different. I knew that, but I didn't want to believe it.'

'But why?' She couldn't let herself believe it. 'Why me?'

'I don't know. Who can explain what causes one person to fall in love with another? I only know I've never felt this way before and while it scares the hell out of me, I don't want to feel any different. I love you, Rachel.'

She stared at him, longing to reach out and touch him, longing for him to kiss her again but terrified that the bubble was going to burst. After all he'd said, could this be real?

'Anyone looking at me would say I have it all,' he continued without false pride. 'Wealth, success, power and a lifestyle where I call all the shots. But I've made a king-size mess of my life and I know it. When I held my son in my arms…' He paused, and now she did reach out, her touch tentative. 'I knew I'd failed him. He was perfect, beautiful and he should have had a life, he should have breathed and laughed and grown up to be a man one day. But I'd been feeling trapped, resenting that I was suddenly thrust into being a husband and father. I hadn't really wanted him until that moment and then it was too late.'

'What happened wasn't your fault, Zac.' She was horrified by the depth of pain in his face. 'It wasn't you who caused it.'

'It felt like it.' He shook his head. 'And there was Moira so sick…I would have done anything to make it right for her, to atone for how I'd felt and our son's death.'

And when that had gone wrong too, he had turned himself into an island, an autonomous being, choosing women of like mind who were content with the super-ficial. 'Oh, Zac.'

'I told you.' He forced a smile that wasn't a smile at all. 'My life's a mess. I'm a mess, deep inside. But I do love you, Rachel. Believe that if nothing else. Over the last couple of weeks that one truth has kept me going.'

She wanted to believe he really loved her, more than anything, but could someone like her ever be enough for someone like him? All her self-doubt and insecurities rose in an overwhelming flood. Shakily, to gain time to bring her chaotic thoughts into order, she murmured, 'Jennie? She knew you'd be here today?'

'Not until this afternoon. I turned up on my aunt's doorstep, knowing you'd said you were spending Christmas with Jennie this year, and threw myself on her mercy. I told her everything, what a fool I'd been and that I loved you, and she suggested I talk to Jennie before she let me stay. She didn't want you upset.' He smiled ruefully. 'Jennie's parents think the world of you, you know. They said you're like one of their own daughters.'

She hadn't known.

'And so I phoned Jennie on her mobile. Apparently the two of you were in a pub, having just had lunch. We talked—at length—and I finally managed to convince her that I was on the level. She ripped a strip off me, I can tell you. A lioness with one cub couldn't have been more fiercely protective.'

Dazedly, she said, 'She didn't say.'

'No, well, she wanted to have a word with me in the flesh before she let me see you. It was along the lines of "You treat her OK or else you'll have me and the rest of the clan to answer to".' He shook his head. 'Formidable lady, my cousin.'

Rachel looked at her hand on his arm, her head spinning.

'You can trust me, Rachel,' he said softly. 'I don't expect you to believe that straight away, not after I've messed up so badly, but let me show you bit by bit. I've told my parents all about you and they want to meet you when you're ready, but there's no rush. I'm staying over here for as long as it takes to gain your trust; I've spent the last week or so putting things in place back home. I haven't taken a proper holiday since goodness knows when so my father agreed he owes me.'

He'd taken her hands in his but she still kept her eyes downcast, fighting with herself, fighting with everything inside her to believe he meant what he was saying. 'Canada's your home,' she managed at last.

'And a beautiful one, you'd love it. But if you want us to live here, that's OK too.'

'Your job, the family firm...'

'My father's able to run the business with a good

manager and he's more realistic than my grandfather was. He knows nothing lasts for ever. It wouldn't break his heart to sell the business one day. And when I was over here at the beginning of December a couple of guys I spoke to put feelers out to see if I was interested in a job, so…' he shrugged '…anything's possible if, *if* you want me.'

If she wanted him? He was holding her hands entwined against his chest and she could feel the steady thump, thump of his heart, smell the clean, sharp scent of his aftershave. She swallowed, gathering all her courage as she met his eyes. 'I couldn't bear it if we got together and one day you fell out of love with me,' she said with simple truth. 'I'd rather have nothing at all than risk that. There's so many lovely women…'

Her face was naked with fear and he gathered her closer, kissing her tenderly. 'I'm a far from perfect male, as I'm sure you've worked out,' he said when his mouth left hers. 'The first part of my life I've made a mess of, and when heaven showed itself I turned tail and ran like a jackrabbit because I hadn't the guts to face up to what was in front of me. Not exactly the greatest confidence-inspiring résumé, I know. But one thing I can promise you is that I'll love you more than life itself until the day I die. I've known lots of other women, Rachel, but none of them have ever touched my heart. To me you're utterly special, adorable, beautiful, unforgettable, and I'll prove it to you for the rest of my life if you'll let me.'

Her senses reeled as she drowned in the gold of his eyes. She could never love anyone like she loved Zac. This was real, this was for ever, and she had to reach out and trust what she was reading in his face. It was all there, the love, the longing and the wonder of it unlocked her voice. 'I love you,' she whispered, shyly almost, 'so much.'

His mouth took hers and, careless of where they were, he kissed her with rising passion, his hands moving over her body as he touched her with hungry, intimate caresses.

'I love you, my darling,' he murmured against her mouth, 'and I know I ought to wait, to give you time to get used to this, but I can't. Will you marry me, Rachel? Will you be my wife, my love, my life?'

He brought a little velvet box out of his pocket and when he clicked it open she saw an exquisite diamond cluster engagement ring nestling in a bed of satin.

The snow was still falling thickly outside the car, but inside, all the joy in the world was concentrated on that one tiny box. 'Yes,' she said, her eyes shining, and he slipped the ring on to her finger where it fitted perfectly. As they did.

It was some time before they left the car and went into the house to find Jennie sitting waiting on the stairs, biting her nails in an agony of impatience. Everyone squealed and cheered and clapped their hands, even the tiny tots who hadn't a clue what was going on but recognised Christmas magic when they saw it. With Zac's arm tightly round her and beaming faces everywhere, for the first time in her life Rachel felt part of a family. Loved, appreciated, wanted.

And later that night, once everyone had retired and they were sitting together in front of the dying fire, loath to part to go to bed, they loved and talked and loved again. 'Our first Christmas together,' Rachel murmured dreamily, glancing down at the glittering diamonds on her left hand, hardly able to believe that everything that had been so wrong was now so right.

'And by next Christmas you'll be an old married lady, perhaps even with a baby on the way,' Zac said huskily.

A baby. Zac's baby. She turned into him, her mouth seeking his, and when the kiss ended they were both breathing hard. She had already decided in her heart that she would move to Canada. There was nothing to hold her here and real friends like Jennie and Susan could come for holidays and she could visit them. Zac's work and family were in Canada and she wouldn't take him away from them.

'Would you object to a winter wedding?' Zac had pulled her onto his lap and she wound her arms around his neck. 'I thought February would give you time to get a dress and I'll find a venue and see to everything. I don't want to wait a day longer than we have to. I want, I *need* to know you're my wife.'

She gazed at him, misty-eyed. 'You're a man of extremes, Zac Lawson.'

'You'd better believe it. I'm going to devote my life to extremely loving you,' he promised softly. 'Starting now.'

And no one could say Zac Lawson wasn't a man of his word.

EPILOGUE

ZAC and Rachel had their winter wedding and everyone said it was the most beautiful day. All their friends and family attended, a huge contingent arriving from Canada. Rachel had been nervous about meeting Zac's parents but she needn't have worried—Zac's father was just like Zac and his mother was the sweetest person and clearly thrilled her son was finally settling down at last.

Rachel had thought long and hard about inviting her mother and sisters: she didn't want the most important day of her life ruined by her mother's spitefulness, but she could hardly invite Lisa and Claire and their families and leave her mother out. In the end, Zac took charge and went to deliver the invitation personally. Exactly what was said that day Rachel never knew and didn't want to know, but on their wedding day her mother behaved impeccably, which was all Rachel wanted.

They honeymooned in the Caribbean for a month and then flew straight to Canada. Rachel fell in love with Zac's house the moment she saw it. It was larger than he'd led her to believe but very private with its own woodland and extensive grounds. Inside, the old mellow oak floors, huge windows with panoramic views over magnificent countryside and massive window seats to curl up on thrilled her.

Zac had given her carte blanche for a complete refurbishment of furniture and fittings if she so wanted, but in the event she changed very little except for adding some feminine touches here and there and changing the colour scheme of the master bedroom from dark coffee and oatmeal to a softer gold and cream.

After a settling-in period when she met Zac's friends and extended family properly and got to know his parents well—his mother was over the moon they were staying in Canada and opened her heart and her home to Rachel as the daughter she'd always wanted but had never had—she applied for, and got, a job as a marketing executive for a fast-food chain. She didn't need to work but she wanted to, and Zac backed her all the way. As he did in everything.

For the first time in her life Rachel knew what it was to have someone who was absolutely hers, who put her first in every regard and who worshipped the ground she walked on. It was heady: it made her feel she could take on the world and win, although the only person she practised her new self-confidence on was her mother. Zac had made it clear to Anne Ellington that if she wanted to stay in contact with them she treat Rachel with the respect he commanded, and Anné complied as meekly as a lamb. In truth, she bathed in the reflected glow of what she saw as Rachel's triumph in making such a wonderful match, boasting to all her friends and neighbours about her daughter's 'handsome millionaire husband'.

Happy months flew by, months of love and laughter and much healing—for both of them. And as Christmas approached, it was decided Jennie and all her family would come over for the holiday, along with Susan and Henry, who were getting married the following spring. Zac's parents' huge, sprawling, colonial-type house could accommodate most of the English guests, but Rachel wanted Jennie and Susan and Henry to stay with them.

And so it was on Christmas Eve, as the five of them sat toasting muffins and eating roast chestnuts in front of the roaring log fire and a red sunset bathed the scene outside the window in a scarlet glow, Rachel took Zac's hand and tapped on her mug of hot chocolate for silence.

'We've an announcement to make.' She looked at Zac and his golden eyes were luminous with love. 'Seven months from now you'd better keep the date clear to come over and see our baby.'

'Rachel!' Jennie and Susan squealed and flung their arms round her while Henry smiled and shook the proud father-to-be's hand, and then it was champagne all round except for Rachel, who was on orange-juice.

Later that night, as Rachel lay curled in Zac's arms in the warm afterglow of their love-making, she felt him stir in his sleep and murmur her name. He often did this, and as always she whispered, 'I'm here,' and watched his handsome, hard face relax and his breathing steady. That he loved her with such a consuming love that even in his sleep he needed reassurance was a miracle to her, but she knew now that to him she was everything.

And she? She was home, at last.

REQUEST YOUR FREE BOOKS!

HARLEQUIN *Presents* ®

2 FREE NOVELS PLUS
2 FREE GIFTS!

PASSION GUARANTEED SEDUCTION

YES! Please send me 2 FREE Harlequin Presents® novels and my 2 FREE gifts (gifts are worth about $10). After receiving them, if I don't wish to receive any more books, I can return the shipping statement marked "cancel." If I don't cancel, I will receive 6 brand-new novels every month and be billed just $4.05 per book in the U.S. or $4.74 per book in Canada. That's a saving of at least 15% off the cover price! It's quite a bargain! Shipping and handling is just 50¢ per book.* I understand that accepting the 2 free books and gifts places me under no obligation to buy anything. I can always return a shipment and cancel at any time. Even if I never buy another book, the two free books and gifts are mine to keep forever.

106/306 HDN E5M4

Name _____ (PLEASE PRINT) _____

Address _____ Apt. # _____

City _____ State/Prov. _____ Zip/Postal Code _____

Signature (if under 18, a parent or guardian must sign)

Mail to the **Harlequin Reader Service:**
IN U.S.A.: P.O. Box 1867, Buffalo, NY 14240-1867
IN CANADA: P.O. Box 609, Fort Erie, Ontario L2A 5X3

Not valid for current subscribers to Harlequin Presents books.

Are you a current subscriber to Harlequin Presents books and want to receive the larger-print edition? Call 1-800-873-8635 today!

* Terms and prices subject to change without notice. Prices do not include applicable taxes. N.Y. residents add applicable sales tax. Canadian residents will be charged applicable provincial taxes and GST. Offer not valid in Quebec. This offer is limited to one order per household. All orders subject to approval. Credit or debit balances in a customer's account(s) may be offset by any other outstanding balance owed by or to the customer. Please allow 4 to 6 weeks for delivery. Offer available while quantities last.

Your Privacy: Harlequin Books is committed to protecting your privacy. Our Privacy Policy is available online at www.eHarlequin.com or upon request from the Reader Service. From time to time we make our lists of customers available to reputable third parties who may have a product or service of interest to you. If you would prefer we not share your name and address, please check here. ☐

Help us get it right—We strive for accurate, respectful and relevant communications. To clarify or modify your communication preferences, visit us at www.ReaderService.com/consumerschoice.

HP10R

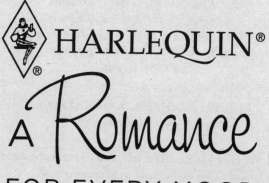

HARLEQUIN®

A Romance

FOR EVERY MOOD™

Spotlight on

Classic

Quintessential, modern love stories
that are romance at its finest.

See the next page
to enjoy a sneak peek from
the Harlequin Presents® series.

*Harlequin Presents® is thrilled
to introduce the first installment of
an epic tale of passion and drama by*
USA TODAY *Bestselling Author*
Penny Jordan!

*When buttoned-up Giselle first meets
the devastatingly handsome Saul Parenti,
the heat between them is explosive....*

"LET ME GET THIS STRAIGHT. Are you actually suggesting that I would stoop to that kind of game playing?"

Saul came out from behind his desk and walked toward her. Giselle could smell his hot male scent and it was making her dizzy, igniting a low, dull, pulsing ache that was taking over her whole body.

Giselle defended her suspicions. "You don't want me here."

"No," Saul agreed, "I don't."

And then he did what he had sworn he would not do, cursing himself beneath his breath as he reached for her, pulling her fiercely into his arms and kissing her with all the pent-up fury she had aroused in him from the moment he had first seen her.

Giselle certainly *wanted* to resist him. But the hand she raised to push him away developed a will of its own and was sliding along his bare arm beneath the sleeve of his shirt, and the body that should have been arching away from him was instead melting into him.

Beneath the pressure of his kiss he could feel and taste her gasp of undeniable response to him. He wanted to devour her, take her and drive them both until they were equally satiated—even whilst the anger within him that she should make him feel that way roared and burned its resentment of his need.

She was helpless, Giselle recognized, totally unable to withstand the storm lashing at her, able only to cling to the man who was the cause of it and pray that she would survive.

Somewhere else in the building a door banged. The sound exploded into the sensual tension that had enclosed them, driving them apart. Saul's chest was rising and falling as he fought for control; Giselle's whole body was trembling.

Without a word she turned and ran.

Find out what happens when Saul and Giselle succumb to their irresistible desire in

THE RELUCTANT SURRENDER

Available January 2011 from Harlequin Presents®

MARGARET WAY

Wealthy Australian, Secret Son

Rohan was Charlotte's shining white knight
until he disappeared—before she had
the chance to tell him she was pregnant.

But when Rohan returns years later as
a self-made millionaire, could the blond,
blue-eyed little boy and Charlotte's heart
keep him from leaving again?

Available January 2011